About the Author

Tarjani Vijaliwala is a masterful storyteller inspired by her lived experiences, from her unconventional upbringing in a coastal town to her curious adventures across the globe. She spent much of her childhood with her nose in a book and loved discovering new, exciting tales of mythological creatures. Now in her late twenties, she has developed the desire to take her imagination to new heights by immortalizing her fantasies in her own written work. And thus began the journey of *Sandsmid…*

Sandsmid: Rise of the Saviour

Tarjani Vijaliwala

Sandsmid: Rise of the Saviour

Olympia Publishers
London

www.olympiapublishers.com
OLYMPIA PAPERBACK EDITION

A CIP catalogue record for this title is
available from the British Library.

ISBN: 978-1-80074-923-8

This is a work of fiction.
Names, characters, places and incidents originate from the writer's
imagination. Any resemblance to actual persons, living or dead, is
purely coincidental.

First Published in 2023

Olympia Publishers
Tallis House
2 Tallis Street
London
EC4Y 0AB

Printed in Great Britain

Dedication

I dedicate this book to my grandfather, who from heaven watches over me. He strongly believed that imagination is the key to a creative mind. To my parents – my father, who is an amazing author himself, always inspired me to write. He is an avid reader himself who allowed me to wander into the world of knowledge where I stumbled upon some life-changing stories. And to my mother, who strongly believed in my potential and never gave up on me even in my darkest of times. I owe everything to you both.

Acknowledgements

I thank my father, Dr I K Vijaliwala, for editing and guiding me through my first book. If you had not written a sequel to your own book for me to find my favourite character again, I would have never been where I am today. Thank you for being with me in every step of my book.

1.

Somewhere Far Away:

The wolves howled. The night seemed too quiet to be true, as if the calm were wrapped all around before a massive storm would break open the roof. The stone walls echoed the cries of the little baby that was held tightly in the arms of a woman. Long black hair, blue almond shaped eyes and a pale complexion, she looked around with dread and then narrowed her eyes in disgust. Things were finally coming into light that maybe her family was not there to help her. There was absolutely no one she could trust now. The flames from the torch illuminated the royal chamber and the red velvet of the plush pillows shone dimly in the mellow light. The woman hugged the baby who suddenly went quiet looking intently at her as if sensing she would be seeing her maybe for the last time.

There was a flash of lightening and the air was brushed by soft tiny snowflakes falling on the windowsill, making their way to establish their territory indicating their stay for quite a season. Sounds of footsteps were heard and a young boy around the age of twelve hustled in trying to keep it as quite as possible. "Your Highness," he said, kneeling in front of the woman. She nodded silently still trying to compose herself from breaking down. "Did you find out everything? Is her life going to be okay there? You always must look after her. You must promise me that you will prepare her for everything lest the time comes." The little boy nodded his head bent low. "Yes, I shall always be with her, around her, but right now I have no other choice. And you are very well aware of that." The woman got stern. Her eyes grew icy cold. "When is the council meeting?" The boy replied, "Tomorrow." The woman asked again, "And what are you going to tell him?" "She went missing." "And her mother got kidnapped," she finished. She gave him a look and he understood. He had always been faithful to her. She had been there for him, looking after him never seeing the difference between a chore boy and her own son if she had one. He took the baby from her hands and turned to leave.

"Wait!" He heard her and stopped. He turned around slowly. "Are they replacing someone in the council?" He answered her by nodding his head into a 'yes'.

"Then I know exactly what to do. Make sure my daughter reaches safely today. I know how to pay you back." The boy shook his head. "You do not need to. I am here because of you, or else I would still be somewhere in the ruins of the village losing my mind." "You take care of my daughter and I will take care of you. Now go. We do not have much time and you have to be back soon." The boy disappeared with the baby. She watched him go wondering how long it will be for the council before they find out about what happened.

***

"We have a crisis, Salvos." The hall was silent. Pin-drop silent. The fire cackled in the furnace and the sound of the waves crashing against the rocks could clearly be heard. Everyone had a dead serious look on their faces. The snow-covered windowpane made a timid screeching noise which otherwise would have been barely audible. The person in the centre looked around sharply when his name was called out. He had pale skin and dark brown eyes. His sharp jawline clearly resembled a bony structure. His eyes narrowed and his face put on a menacingly calm expression. All the other four people looked at him immediately dreading his building anger, getting all anxious. He cleared his throat.

"I know we have a crisis. But there absolutely no one to take his place. Or at least qualified enough to take his place. I respected Edward. Although his ways of working were always different, his efficiency was what kept the Desert locked and safe. Now I am worried. If we do not find any suitor, the level is going to be exposed to all kinds of unpredictable danger."

"I hope we are not just going to discuss the dangers, but also find a solution to fix this." The guy on the left said. He was bald, with narrow eyes and a thin lean face that was always frowning. Salvos looked at him sharply. "Volt, I know I am getting to that. Be patient." The poison in his tone made Volt withdraw. He watched Salvos take a deep breath and then continue, "My wife and I decided that the rightful heir to his position would be his own son." The members around the table looked at each other and started talking in hushed whispers. Salvos narrowed his eyes smirking. "Silence!" Everyone went quiet.

A huge guy on the far end of the table with white hair and kind eyes looked Salvos in the eye and said, "I agree with you, but he is just a boy. How will he know the politics of the bridge?"

Salvos looked at him with a calm expression. "I know,

Breeman. I will personally see to it and send him to you, Reh," he said pointing at the guy seated third next to him. He had long silver hair and extremely handsome features. His white teeth gleamed in the mundane lighting of the hall. He nodded. "I shall take care of him. For now, let that boy breathe for a while and enjoy his age. Soon he is going to see some things that he is not going to be fond of. Which reminds me, the Siren week is coming up, do you have her for the sacrifice?"

Salvos took a deep breath before answering. "My wife took care of her extra well. She is going to be fully healthy for our sacrifice," he said without any hints of regret or sadness. Breeman looked uncomfortable. "Salvos are you sure? She is your own daughter."

Salvos raised his hand to silence him. "She was given to us by Siren herself so that when the right time comes, we return the favour and regain our power. She was born for this job." Breeman knew that arguing any further would cost him his life. He looked down with sadness dreading the crime he had to be a part of.

Salvos spoke again, "The session is over my fellow members. I would now go and check on my daughter and wife and we shall all meetup on the day of the ceremony. Everything should hopefully be ready by the keepers." He got up. So did the others. One by one everyone left the hall, and the lights went out.

The corridors echoed with the loud footsteps. Salvos walked swiftly on the cold stone flooring his feet rhythmically tapping on the stones creating the echo that sounded of urgency. 'Tap, tap, tap, tap'. The rooms he passed by remained closed with dark wooden doors looming over the narrow space. The torches burned bright casting dancing shadows over the walls on the other side. Salvos quickened his pace. Something did not seem right. His wife would usually come out to greet him by the time he is back from his sessions. They had to come up with the ceremonial outfit for their daughter. Although defiant in the beginning she had reluctantly agreed to his demand of sacrificing their own daughter. The extreme silence and no sound of her singing to their daughter was something that he was not expecting.

He turned at the corner and entered the unusually dark room. He walked out and pulled a torch from the wall and got inside the room again and screamed in anger.

***

Several Years Later Somewhere in Toronto, Canada

"Were you up last night?" Adrian asked Trinity as they were working out in the school gym. Trinity, in the middle of her push-ups, looked at him with a wary eye and nodded. Adrian got up from his seat nearby and walked towards her. His tall, six feet lean physique with a perfectly squared jawline and green eyes were the reason a lot of girls lost their focus during their workouts. His face had a frown as he approached her. "This is not good for your training. You need to catch up on your sleep."

Trinity sighed. The dreams had been haunting her again. The same dreams that she used to have as a child were coming back. She went back to her workout. Adrian had been training her for combat skills and she regretted to this day as to why she had signed up for that training in the first place. She got up all sweaty and walked towards the cabinet to grab her sipper and slipped on the wet spot. Before she could fall Adrian came and grabbed her. "Hey there, easy, you are fragile enough. I do not want you breaking your bones now." Trinity rolled her eyes and ignored him.

"Why do not you finally tell him you like him instead of giving him excuses to grab you," Kyla, her rival classmate sneered from behind her. Adrian looked at her sharply, "Mind your own business, roach." Kyla made a face at him. Trinity looked down with flushed cheeks and walked out of the gym.

"Hey Trinity, wait!" Adrian chased after her. "What's wrong with you? Is something really bothering you then I would like to know that. I am your best friend, man."

Trinity took a deep breath. Her five-foot six figure shaking slightly in her two-piece gym outfit turned towards him. Her mid-length dyed brown hair all sweaty and tied in her loose ponytail contrasted with her beautiful blue eyes and plump red lips as she opened them to answer back to Adrian. "Listen, boo, I have been having some rough time lately. I just want to be left alone for a while. So, see you in class?" she said with a blank look on her face.

Adrian gave up. "Sure, see you in marketing management." Saying this he walked back to the gym. Trinity kept walking towards her locker with her head down and bumped into a guy coming out of the class carrying a box of magazines, causing him to drop the box. "Hey, watch out where you're going."

Trinity jerked up. "Sorry." And bent down to help him pick up the magazines off the floor. While putting them in the box she noticed a small picture of five wolves that caught her eye and below that was written, 'The warning signs for a bad omen. Know your strategies.' She tore her glance away from that and handed him the last copy and went to her locker.

Her best friend Aella stopped next to her. Her dark red hair, her tiny little body with her too big for her face black gleaming eyes looked up at her in excitement. "Last day of the semester and tomorrow we are off! Yay."

Trinity snapped her locker shut and forced a smile. "Yeah looking forward to that." Aella narrowed her gaze. "Hey, you have not been sleeping. What is with you? Is it the same dream again?" Trinity looked at her questioningly. Aella shrugged. "Adrian told me who else?" Trinity nodded. "I do not understand. The sleeping pills given to me should be working, but recently they are not. This is the second time I have been getting this dream in two days. And all this started after my twenty-fourth birthday."

Aella looked at her with concern. "You think it has to do with some hidden magic powers that needed to be awakened at this age?" Trinity looked at her seriously before realising it was a joke. She struck Aella with her bag jokingly. "It's not funny, babe, I keep on seeing this woman, and it's been haunting me. I felt the same when..." Her voice trailed off.

Trinity and Aella felt silent. Aella put a hand on her shoulder while Trinity tried to compose herself. The memory of her abusive parents till she was eighteen. The worse was when they beat her up with a belt just for falling asleep on the dinner table and then locking her up in the basement. The school board found out the next day and decided to shift her with a foster family. Their beatings still echoed in her head and after that for a few years she would wake up in the middle of the night screaming. Her foster family did not really give a shit about her. But if they minded their own business, Trinity was cool with it. She brushed off these thoughts and composed herself to go to the class with Aella.

Trinity, Aella and Adrian sat deliberately on the last of the seats by the end of the classroom so Aella could eat. Adrian pulled out his laptop and, pretending to take notes of whatever the professor said, started gaming silently. Trinity tried hard to focus on whatever Mr Leo was saying about the marketing branches until her eyes started drooping. Soon she felt everything go black.

"Bluebee, can you hear me? You have only a quarter left. Please come back to me, baby. I miss you. I do not have much time. Do not ignore me. We need you. Come." And the blue-eyed woman's smile faded a little as she held out her hand towards her. "In fact, we do not have much time. Hurry!"

"Trinity Dominique Woods," Aella whispered loudly shaking her with apparent exasperation. Trinity got up groggily to see Mr Leo still rattling on about the branches without noticing anything. She tried to sit up straight and stifled a yawn. Adrian leaned over with a warm look. "I know whatever it is Trinity, I will help you out of it. Just wait till we reach 'Happy days'."

Happy days was their vacation place in the woods of beautiful Alberta. Trinity and Aella were going to drive there the following day, while Adrian had to finish off his elective extra assignment and drive on his own the day after. They all got up to leave the class, where Adrian waved them a goodbye.

Aella looked at Trinity before heading off in another direction. "I'll come to pick you up tomorrow at eight in the morning. Be ready with everything okay? And do not forget my cigarette box. I left it at your place." Trinity nodded meekly. "Hey, it's going to be fun, all right. You're going to get through this," Aella said putting an emphasis on everything. Trinity smiled at her and walked away.

She reached home and started packing. Maybe something

good will happen. Maybe she could get rid of whatever or whoever she was dreaming about. Hopeful, she began filling her bag.

***

Only a few hours left for the final submission for the semester. Adrian wiped the sweat off his forehead as he tried to keep his focus maintained. He could have asked for help from any of his friends but oh well, anyway the system for the online submissions sucked. His literature knowledge was far better than the updated registries full of the collected data for the library, but nervousness was his trait. His anxious fingers tapped on the 'send' button, watching the flashing 'sent' message on his screen. He relaxed for a bit.

His phone rang. Looking at the name, he sighed. Plans for the vacation. He looked at the name. Trinity. He picked up the call and answered, "Yeah I know I will drive safely. I will see you guys tomorrow. Bye."

He looked at his packed outfits. He had already rented his car and sat down on the table again to calculate his moves. Not much time left and much to his distaste, Aella was also joining them. Not that he didn't like her, but she was never the part of the plan. He swallowed hard. He really couldn't do anything about it. They were best friends in school after all. Closing his suitcase, he picked up his big fat leather diary from the table and stuffed it in his backpack. All that was left to do now was to just wait for the right time to drive.

2.

On the Way to Alberta

Trinity pressed hard on the gas paddle. The roads were empty, and the speed limit made them smile. If there was anything that made her happy that day was to be able to drive at her desirable speed. She switched on the car radio.

"Easy, miss, I still haven't paid the full amount for this car," Aella said playfully sitting next to her. She was the shotgun, but Trinity took it upon herself to change the music. The weather broadcast was very much like bright and sunny for the entire day. The fields gave way to dense trees and beautiful lakes. A fresh cool breeze blew in from the window making them breathe in the clean air.

"Sorry," Trinity mumbled slowing down the speed. Aella laughed. "You know you do not have to apologise for everything. You can sometimes stand up for yourself." Trinity gave her a side glance before answering, "If I ever would have stood up for myself before, I would already have been dead. Anytime I would say no to something, they would hit me." Aella put a comforting hand on her. "Hey, it's the past. Do not let it ruin your present. Do not let it cloud your strong beautiful personality." Trinity smiled. She knew she was blessed to have Aella on her side at any time. She thanked her stars for it before replying, "I shall try, but I definitely do not understand how to stop this weather cloud such a bright sunny day."

Aella squinted in the bright light and then her brows shot up. "Holy cow, are those the clouds I see? They are so dark. I just hope it doesn't start raining before we make it. It would be so difficult to drive then."

They both looked as they were quickly approaching the cloudy area where suddenly out of nowhere their car plunged into thick fog. It was thicker than they had anticipated, and Trinity could see absolutely nothing ahead. The radio frequency started fluctuating and the car components started behaving as if they were alive and refusing to function but still working against their own will. Aella sat up straight, now a little scared. "Trinity, what's going on?" Trinity looked around in confusion and then ahead into the thick white curtain. "I have no idea, girl. I think I should pull over to the side before we crash into something." "Good call, but do you know exactly where is the side right now? Because if not we might get the car off the tracks and drown into the lake who knows." Trinity asked her, "So what should we do? I think we should just keep driving slowly until we get out of this. I will keep the headlights on high beam." Aella nodded nervously.

Trinity switched to a high beam and continued at a minimal speed, hoping to get out of the fog any minute. But the curtain of white just got thicker. Trinity felt the steering wheel jerking slightly in her hands getting warmer than usual. Before she could turn to Aella and tell her about it, she heard a horrified squeal. Aella was gagging trying to get some air. She was utterly in dismay as to what was happening. Trinity grabbed the bottle of water from the holder near her and held it out to Aella. "It's going to be fine. Drink some water. We are nearly there." Aella took the bottle looking at her questioningly, 'Are we?', and drank some water before looking at Trinity again and gasping in horror. "What? Did you see something?" Trinity whirled around, to see outside the car window but there was nothing. She turned back to see Aella pointing at her. Trinity felt something wet on her face. She wiped it with her hand and then saw it. Blood. She was having a nosebleed. Trinity never had a nosebleed, except that one time in childhood, when her mother threw a pan on her face, which almost broke her nose. Even though, that wasn't a normal nosebleed, the memory of it still gave her shivers. Trinity frantically started looking for tissues, wiping her nose, wondering what might have caused it. Balancing the steering wheel with one hand and holding a tissue over her nose with the other, she hoped they would get out of this cursed fog soon. Aella found her voice and spoke the exact same thought. "I think this fog has something to do with all this."

Trinity pressed on the pedal harder. The sooner they get out of it the better. She sped up a little more. Aella had gotten quiet. No one was saying anything, hoping to see the fog thinning. Soon enough, after a long time, they could see the white curtain getting thinner. They could make out green in the distance and Aella let out a sigh of relief. The fog grew thinner and thinner and finally they both could see a dense dark forest looking down upon them, ahead. However, the weather had turned extremely gloomy, with dark clouds just waiting for the right time to break open. Thunder rumbled somewhere in the distance.

Aella groaned. "No, this was supposed to be HAPPY DAYS, there is absolutely nothing happy about this weather. And I feel so drained." Trinity looked at her and remained silent. She too was feeling drained. And nauseous. The sooner they get to the place, the better it was for them.

It was their first time driving on these roads, so they did not exactly know where they were supposed to go for their stay. 'Happy Days' on the phone had showed the same location they were currently in, earlier. Trinity got out her phone again, to check for further directions. Handing the phone over to her partner, Trinity stopped abruptly in front of a roughly carved wooden stop sign. Someone had written something in bold letters below it, 'Trespassers shall be prosecuted'.

Aella looked up. "Trespassing for what?" Trinity shrugged. "I do not know. It might be just because of the storm or heavy rainfall; the forest might be risky." "But risky for what?" "I do not know Aella, I do not think we were warned about any of this by our agency when we booked the place. Did you find the location?" Aella held up the phone. "No internet bars. I hope you have the route memorised." Trinity shook her head almost giving up. "This is all so messed up. Try doing it from your phone." Aella took out hers from the charging and immediately dropped it. "My, my, it's burning hot," she said, trying to hold the phone again. "Trinity, I do not think it's a good idea, I feel it's getting hotter and hotter." Saying this she rolled down the car window and was shook by a chilling breeze. She held her phone again. "It's weird, it's like someone lit it on fire," she said looking at it in shock seeing flames come out of her phone. "Aella watch out!" Trinity slapped her hand so hard that it threw her phone out of the window. Before any of them could react further, they heard a small exploding noise and got outside the car to see her phone in flames on the ground. Aella put both her hands on her head and wailed, "Perfect, now what?"

Trinity stood there for a while. Then she got close to the sign and started looking around. Fat raindrops started hitting her face. She could make out wide spaces on the sides of the sign from where the vehicles could pass through. At least it was wide enough for their car to pass. Going back in this weather seemed like 'not a good' idea for now. She and Aella hurried back into the car and turned the heater on. "I do not think finding a gas station right now would be a smart idea." Aella nodded. "My phone died and yours doesn't work. The weather is crappy and if we go back, we might have to go through that bitch of a fog again. This place anyway looks like the place we were going to go. Should we just drive through from the side of that sign?"

Trinity thought for a minute. "I mean even if we do get in trouble, someone would have to come and tell us that, and we could use them for help. Let us just do it." Taking the control of the wheel again, she drove from right beside the sign, entering the murky grounds, the engine roaring harder plunging into the dark woods. Trinity drove blindly for a while in the thick raindrops, and then spotted a faint light on the left side of the road. Aella too must have noticed it as well because she sat up with her hands on the dashboard, eager to look for a ray of hope. Trinity followed the light and soon they were pulling up outside a nice big forest cottage. The light was coming from the lamppost outside the porch. They stared at the cottage from inside of their car for a while before Aella spoke, "This looks so much like the one we booked, do not you think?" Trinity nodded. "I do not think we should get that excited about it though. Let us get out and check first." Aella questioned, "What if it's dangerous? Shouldn't we stay locked inside?"

"Right outside the house in the middle of the forest? I do not think so. The gas might run out any minute." Aella was still uncertain. "But we can stay in the car till morning and then drive back again?" Trinity thought for a while. Aella's argument did make sense.

They both agreed to stay in the car. After a while Aella attempted to start a conversation to kill time. "So why do you think all those weird things happened in that fog?"

Trinity shrugged. "I do not know honestly. But I have read that sometimes these things happen if there are fluctuations in an energy field." Aella nodded. They sat in silence again for a while.

"Screw it. I'm going out for a smoke," Aella said getting out of the car. "I do not think that's a great idea, let alone a safe one." Aella rolled her eyes at her. "As if we have something better to do. I am not going to explore the forest."

"All right fine. But stay within the vicinity." Aella nodded and pointed at the porch.

"I will stay right in front of your eyes." Saying this, she walked close to the lamppost near the porch and pulled out a cigarette. Trinity took out her phone and switched it off and on in the hope to get a signal.

"Trinity!" Trinity jerked up at the sound of her best friend calling. "You scared me. What!"

Aella gestured her to come out of the car. "Come, look."

Without thinking she got out of the car and ran towards Aella. She looked at where she had been pointing. Footsteps. Going inside the house through the front door. They were clearly visible and wet against the wooden floor. Aella whispered, "You think someone must have gone inside the house just before we came? Should we knock?"

Trinity shook her head and replied with caution, "No, let us not take that risk. Let us go back to the car and lock the doors from inside. It is better to stay here then venture in the dark forest, that is why I insist on keeping our car parked here rather than some place where there is absolutely no light. We can think about something in the morning."

Aella stood there thinking for a second before answering, "You're right. Let us go back."

Just as they turned, a hooded figure appeared in front of them. "Too late," it said, and then everything happened way too fast. Trinity felt a heavy blow, heard Aella's faded screams and then everything went black.

***

On the Other Side in the Same Land

The walls dripped bright red and the hall smelled flames. In a brightly lit corner in that hall, a tiny little woman paced around nervously. She was short and thin, with a dark complexion and bright yellow short hair. She would shake her head in some sort of denial, every few seconds.

A tall dark man with a shaved head sat on a velvet armchair, his long cloak touching the carpet. Even though the torches in the room were bright yellow, the room had a reddish orange glow to it, the walls inside being red. They could hear the wind rustling outside in the dunes. The heat because of the hot sand would have been unbearable, but the house they were in was designed to keep the interior cool. The lady shook her head again. The tall man rolled his eyes at her. She stopped and said to him nervously, "He got her, Salem, but I do not think they would last long before getting caught."

Salem got up from his chair. He appeared to be towering over a small creature. The lady craned her neck to look at his face. "You need to take it easy. I have suggested a perfect place. I do not think they would be detected easily. They need to make it out to that range fast. If at all Salvos gets a wind of it."

The lady shuddered. "You know he has been furious since like forever now. I do not know what the news of an intruder breaching the border would be like to him. He tends to lash out his anger at anyone these days. How do they still have him in the board?"

Salem shrugged. "That is what we are fighting for now right? Justice. We need the right people in the board. Not the ones who take revenge for their personal issues. That is why I like to stay away from these politics. As for now, all we can do is just to sit calm and hope they made it on time."

The winds grew louder. The woman looked at Salem and then at her feet and then back at him, "I just hope our message is read and interpreted in Midland. I know someone there, who is more trustworthy than anyone I know over here."

Salem walked to the nearby table, which was laden with multiple parchments and leather diaries and pulled out a clean roll. He handed it to the woman and said, "You know what to write to them when you get to Midland. I am going to stay here and make sure no one finds out this little secret. But I can arrange for you to leave right now if you want to. And I want you to meet my daughter when you reach there."

She nodded. "It might take me some time to reach there. Watch out for them, Salem. I do not think we still have the right information. I heard that someone has just been added to the number."

Salem frowned. "Are you sure?" She shrugged. Beads of sweat broke against his forehead. He knew something was not right and it was too late for them to intervene and stop the plan. He looked at her in dismay and said in a shaky voice, "If that's the case then we need to save that extra person's life before it is too late."

3.

"Oomph, where the hell are, we?" Trinity could hear Aella's pained muffled voice from nearby. She tried to open her eyes but kept them closed as she felt her head spinning. She felt herself moving and figured she might be in the backseat of a car. "Wait a minute," she thought, wondering how in the first place did she get there. Slowly the incident before she passed out replayed inside of her head. She had been knocked out by someone in a hood and probably they are in that very someone's car right now. That meant for only one possibility. They had been kidnapped. Kidnapped! She shot up and sat straight in her seat, her head wobbly again. She looked on her side, Aella holding her head in her arms apparently trying to process everything.

Trinity noticed they had not been tied. She looked at Aella. She was free of any bindings as well. The roads were dark and there were no streetlights to be seen anywhere. She reached out her hand and poked Aella on her shoulders. She groaned. "What?" She tried to turn her head, but it was obvious it hurt because of all the efforts she made to do it.

"Aella what's going on?"

"I will tell you what's going on," the guy in the driving seat replied. Trinity noticed that he was still wearing the hoodie and his voice was deep and croaky but oddly familiar. They were in the backseat of their own car which was reverberating violently. "I have kidnapped you both, but it is only for your own best interests. Do not try to strangle me and take the wheel because if you do, you will not know the way to get out of here. Just sit tight." He added as the car bounced to another bump. Trinity sat quietly. The bumpy ride was enough to make her feel sick and weak. Her stomach rumbled. She realised she hadn't had any food in the last twenty-four hours. She rested her head back on the seat and looked outside the window.

The roads appeared to be getting rockier and it felt as if they were going up a mountain. The trees started getting sparse and the wind caught up speed. At some point the car swayed so dangerously, getting really close to the edge of the road from which she could see the valley, that if that driver lost control at any moment, they could plummet to their deaths.

Aella groaned again. "Where are we going?" Trinity looked at her and made a gesture to ask her to remain silent. Aella rolled her eyes and closed them exhaling loudly. Trinity continued to stare out of the window once again trying to rack her brains as to where she had heard the hoodie's voice before. She thought maybe if she worked up a bit she would be able to grab the guy by his neck and ask him to turn the car around, but as she tried getting up, she gave up as every limb in her body was asking her to take rest. She killed that thought. She was too weak to fight anyone right now.

The way ahead suddenly got smoother and Trinity felt that they night be driving on a concrete road. Big limestone structures started appearing on each side on the road and then she noticed. A huge dilapidated looking castle looming ahead of them.

They were speeding past the open gates of the castle when the weather started getting intensely stormy again. It was already dark outside, but Trinity felt that because of the amount of time that had passed, it must be getting close to dawn. The tiny dim light at the end of the road somehow made the daunting house a little welcoming. The guy was still driving in silence and the car entered a space that looked like a huge cave.

The car stopped with a jolt. Aella almost broke her nose while getting pushed forward in her seat. The guy in the front got out and opened the door for Trinity to get out. Aella followed the pursuit and they stood there outside, weak, tired and exhausted trying to make out who the guy was. His back was towards them, but his eerily familiar voice echoed in the semi-darkness of the cave. "Follow me," he said and started walking ahead. They got into another small passage through a tiny wooden ledge door. Aella tried to catch a glimpse of his face but it was still too dark to determine his features.

They got on a spiral staircase that appeared to be endless. Finally entering a bigger room, carved inside a stone cliff, they walked on and on until they reached a spacious ballroom. It was lit with torches on all the sides, with paintings lining up the walls.

"Welcome to the Senge Castle, ladies. I never knew I would be able to fulfil this almost impossible task." Saying this, the guy turned towards them and took off his hood.

Aella gave a timid scream and Trinity just stared at him in disbelief. "ADRIAN?"

***

They were surprised yet shocked to see their friend. However, he did not seem so happy to see them. He had a serious face, and his eyes looked tensed. "I'm afraid that was the only way to get you guys here. I'm sorry for hurting you."

Aella crossed her arms and grit her teeth. "I mean we TOTALLY wouldn't have believed you right? If you would just have asked us to come with you without hitting our heads and making us feel all woozy." She swallowed a lump.

Trinity looked at him seriously. "Adrian she's right. All you could just have done is ask us to come with you. You needn't have gone through all that trouble just to get us here."

Adrian stood motionless with a hint of sadness in his eyes. He quickly rearranged his features and said, "I knew you would say that, but if at all the army saw that I brought two living people with me through the border I do not think you both would have been actually alive. You had to be kept off the radar, and I had to ensure it stays that way till I get us on the way to the 'safe house'. The roads have yet not been kept on a surveillance, so it was okay for you guys to actually 'sit' on your seats."

"Well you could have just asked us to duck under the seats if you really wanted," Aella said, frustrated, throwing her hands in the air. "And what's with all this 'safe house' and army?"

Adrian replied, "That is why I expected you to not believe me. And I was ordered to get you out of there before you get trapped. I had been working on this for days. I am, however, not allowed to give you more information on your whereabouts, just know that you are safer here than where you were before."

Aella made a dash for the front doors and tried to yank on the huge metal handle. Trinity stood there trying to figure out what exactly was going on, but exhaustion and the throbbing head were taking a toll over her brain. Adrian looked disapprovingly at Aella. "You cannot escape this place. Try as you might, you won't be able to get out of here."

After quite some trying, she gave up and stood next to them

looking around. Trinity scanned her surroundings. The hall was a smooth double height with a crystal chandelier hanging from the ceiling. The walls adorned beautiful paintings, some of which were starting to peel off and a long wooden corridor that ended in a magnificent staircase covered with a dusty red carpet ended a few feet off from where they were standing.

Trinity looked at Adrian. "Listen, you have always been there for me. I trust you. Whatever you are up to, I know it is for the best. Just tell me where we are and where is this 'safe house' we are in exactly located?"

A slight wave of relief appeared to pass on his face. "Trinity and Aella, we are in Senge, the capital of Sandsmid. Do not ask me for more, it would hurt me for not being able to give you the answers."

Aella rolled her eyes. Trinity showed him an understanding nod. "I understand you guys must be exhausted and starving. I will show you your room." Saying this, Adrian started walking up the staircase. Aella and Trinity followed.

Trinity stumbled on the way, extremely tired and cold. The place was cold and deserted. It appeared so lonely and abandoned, as if no one had been trading on their paths, for at least a hundred years. As they walked, the corridors looked dark and there were green flames erupting from the torches on the walls. The narrow dimly lit corridors did look scary and slightly damp. Trinity sniffed. She felt as if they had been used more frequently than the main hall. Finally, they reached a large wooden door, where Adrian pulled out a skull key and inserted it into the keyhole and pushed the door open to reveal a large living room, with a fireplace and plush red couches, followed by two bedrooms on it's either side for both the ladies.

The best part of the entire day, however, was the sight of

the heavy trays laden with food on the large wooden table in their living room. Aella rushed to that table. Trinity, without thinking much as well ran to the table and filled her plate with pretty much everything that was there. A large pile of steaming mashed potatoes, baguettes, garlic bread, tomato soup, cheese and bread sticks, jars of orange juice and fresh strawberries with cream. Adrian looked at them stuffing themselves without taking any notice of his presence, he smiled and silently turned back and left the room. Trinity saw him leave but ate her food in silence. A part of her was still mad at how he had acted whether for their good or their bad in the last few hours.

After a heavy meal, Aella went into her bedroom and Trinity flopped on her bed and fell asleep almost instantly. Everything felt calm and peaceful for once, at that moment.

***

Underground near Senge, in the Tunnels

Angelica flipped through the pages on the rosewood table, anxiously. Her dark green eyes nearly watered, as she kept on staring at an open parchment roll continuously before finally tearing her gaze away. She stopped, tied her loose flashy red long hair into a bun and went back to studying the roll again.

The levels were described in a way that she was certain no one had ever seen before. The rules of the bridges undermined the rules written in this parchment. Something was not right. She had been studying the ways of the bridge council for years. Every level was kept perfectly distinct and isolated from the other. There was no way the parchment could be proven correct.

Her glance darted around the empty cave nervously before

going back to studying the roll again. She felt the need of hiding this one important documentation before it went into the wrong hands. Whoever was working towards making a move, by the description in this roll, had to be doing it quickly. They had almost no time left. Summer Equinox was around the corner and she knew the bridges came for the sacrificial ceremony in the 'void'.

She fumbled around for a quill and some ink and started noting down the details of the parchment in a small leather notebook. She could not believe whatever was written in it and continued casting cautious glances around her while copying the information. There was a sketch of a star-shaped amulet inside that roll. She wondered aloud, "What do they mean by opening the levels for everyone? We have an enemy ahead." Realising she had said it out loud, she went back to writing again.

"It means that we must fight against the bridge first."

Angelica stopped and stood up, alert. She looked around but the sound was coming from behind a corner in the far end, where she couldn't clearly see. Her hand slowly wrapped around her katana, which was resting peacefully in its studded sheath around her waist. "Who is it?" she asked in a shaky voice. "I know you are no army, but you can still be a threat. Face me and leave or die and you shall never be found by anyone dear to you."

"It's okay, Angelica, I'm not here to fight. I'm here to tell the place you should go looking for more information. The temple." Surprised to hear her name, Angelica's grip around her katana eased a little, but she still held on to it. As she looked, a short woman with bright yellow hair calmly walked towards her.

Angelica had never seen her before. She asked in a tense tone, "Who are you? What do you want from me?"

The woman smiled at her. "I see you are exactly as you were described to me. I have a plan. If we become allies, I know the way to reach the 'void'."

Angelica stopped and stared at her. This woman felt like she was talking sensible. She asked, "And why should I trust you? You could be a spy."

The woman laughed. "Trust me, I am not. Salem sent me."

*

In the Safe House

The howling sounds were getting louder. The wolves circled around Trinity while she felt herself weak in the knees. Her legs seemed to have turned to jelly. The cliff edge was just a few steps behind her, and the wolves were just a foot away from pouncing on her and gobbling her up. Suddenly, a little black wolf from the pack decided to stop the growling and speak to her in a deep groggy voice, "Trinity, you will find us every time we feel that something is not right. Do not trust the scene, trust your heart. The cliff may look like it's going to be your death, but it is the grounds that can kill. The one you are next to shall not be trusted." And then, all the wolves stopped growling and joined the little black wolf in singing something in a low growling note that roughly sounded like,

"We know, we know, we know you from the start
You little one by blood, and a sengee by heart,
Trust no one with a cape, a mane and a hat
We brought you from your world,

But you belonged here before that,
Stories shall reveal, the wounded and the healed,
There is much more to that,
From what you see, all that is sealed,
We will leave you for now,
But we will come back before dawn"

Trinity woke up with a start. She ran a sweaty hand to her temples, where it hurt. The pain passed and she weirdly remembered the dream clearly. The thunder cackled and she wondered how many hours she had been asleep for. The storm must have gotten worse. She clutched her blankets hard around her and decided to reiterate everything that had been happening with her and Aella after they drove through that fog. Everything had happened so fast it got all blurred when she tried to think about it. Not able to sleep any longer, she decided to take a walk and explore the place. 'Trust Adrian, my foot! That moron got us to a strange place. I hope there are no psychopaths in this house,' she thought before creeping out of her bed and walking out of her room into those dark and damp corridors.

The walls were partially lit by the torches. Crystal chandeliers hung over the stone flooring and the corridors stretched out infinitely. Trinity treaded as quietly as possible. She could still hear the rain pounding against the glass windows somewhere in the distance. There were no intersecting hallways or more rooms other than her room. 'So, what is behind these long walls?' she wondered, walking. The stretched-out corridor finally ended when she reached an intersection that was even more dimly lit than that damp corridor.

The hallway had dark furniture and big paintings of stunning women on the walls. Trinity felt that somehow, the resemblance of all those women in the paintings that she could make out in the semi-light was similar. They were all smiling, and Trinity felt a rush of warm soothing feeling that made her feel safe and secure for the first time since they had arrived. She reached a spiral staircase that descended into the darkness below, but she still made her way carefully downstairs.

She was feeling all brave and adventurous now.

She noticed she was in a big room that too was lit with two torches. The windows on one side were large and she could see nothing but the dark cloudy sky through the thick raindrops. The furniture in the room was minimal and dark, just like upstairs and there were more paintings of the similar looking women on one wall. She saw a small four-poster bed and a small table and chair on to its side. A large old wardrobe stood on one side of the room. It was so big, that it took almost one-fourth of that wall.

Something on the table caught her eye. A lonely looking book on an empty table. She got closer to it and picked it up. It had a title. 'The rules of the bridge.'

She opened the book and saw some pretty scribbles on the first page. One line written in there, caught her attention,

"It's so hard to believe but every time someone enters our Sandsmid, they never understand that it is impossible to get out from here." – *Haseena*

4.

Senge Safe House:

The writing on the paper looked old, but it pretty much drained all the blood from Trinity's face. If that was the case, then Adrian better be telling the truth. From her dreams and Adrian's confession, one thing that was clear was, they were probably on the other side of some veil that was hiding this world from their own. It was hard for her to think a lot about it at present, but she was sure she needed to snoop around more for some answers. And if Adrian was someone's minion and doing their dirty work, she'd better keep everything to herself till she for sure knew what exactly Sandsmid was and it was indeed some 'new world' she was hearing about and not some drug lord's house in a forest retreat.

Keeping her strong, she took the book in her hand and started going up the stairs. She wanted to get back to her room before anyone could find out that she was out of her bed, especially not if that anyone was a psychopath's minion. It wasn't hard for her to find the corridor she came from, thanks to those portraits of those stunning women and absolutely no rooms and stretched-out corridors. She finally made her way back to the large wooden doors of her room, but not before hearing faint footsteps in the distance. She got inside her bedroom and climbed onto her bed and drifted into an uncomfortable sleep.

She woke up at the sound of Aella yelling her name out in annoyance. She smiled at her as she opened her eyes. At least one person she could trust for now. Remembering the previous night, the footsteps she heard at the end nagged her. Aella must have read her uncomfortable expression and asked, "You had nightmares about your parents?" Trinity shook her head and smiled, "On the contrary, I had a nice dream for once." Aella smiled at her comfortingly. Trinity wondered, how she could have come across such an understanding, loving friend who despite of knowing her rough history, always tried to make her feel better.

Trinity saw lights flooding in through the living room. "Is it noon now? I thought I slept forever. What is the time?" she asked Aella, stretching. "No, I guess it's still night. The hallways are rightly lit. I wonder how many hours we have actually slept." There was a soft knock at the door. "Ah, there comes Adrian, let us ask him."

Adrian walked into the room wearing a grey silk night robe looking sleepy. "What's up, fam?" he asked yawning. "Adrian, I feel like I have slept forever, why isn't it morning yet?" Trinity asked him. He stood there for a while sleepily looking at them trying to stifle another yawn and then replying, "Because here we never had a morning, or let me rephrase it, we never saw morning light like back in your world. I do not remember seeing light here since I was born. It has always been like this."

Trinity remained silent at this. Something about her dream from the previous night troubled her. The wolves had told her about it. She racked her brains against her faint memory of that dream to find out what they had said related to this place. 'We shall be back before dawn.' She kept that to herself. If there was no dawn in this place, what kind of a place was this?

Aella however had a question to his answer. "What do you mean since you were born? You were born at this haunted retreat? And what do you mean by no 'morning light'? Adrian, how you brought us to a strange science experiment island?"

Adrian smiled. He looked at them as if he did understand their curiosity but answered otherwise, "I will tell you everything shortly. Technically it is morning, so we have breakfast ready downstairs. You are going to meet two new people down there. They are like my family and will help me keep you guys safe. We will work out the entire plan as we are running short on time."

Hoping to get some clarity over the situation, Trinity and Aella got dressed to go downstairs. As soon as they reached the main hall, Adrian, who was already waiting for them, led them to a big dining hall. It had an entirely open front side that overlooked a beautiful courtyard. It was still stormy, but the courtyard looked magnificently bright. Two people were already seated by the time they arrived. One was working on something in his book. He looked muscular and lean with sharp handsome features. His thick blond hair clashed with his thin eyebrows. He smiled slightly and nodded in acknowledgement at the ladies and went back to doing whatever he had been engrossed in before. The other guy looked simply ordinary with almond eyes, brown hair and a pale complexion. He appeared fully dedicated to whatever he was eating but got up to greet the ladies introducing himself as Michael. The other guy who was working in his book probably felt embarrassed by his ignorant behaviour and got up to greet the ladies as well. He introduced himself as Samaar. He further mentioned, "Adrian filled us in on everything. I know you guys have been looking for answers. We will try our best to give you as much information as possible."

Trinity nodded and smiled at him. They all sat down to eat. The food looked delicious. There were small mountains of strawberries and sugared whipped cream. There were glasses with fresh juice and the plates were already laden with different food like mashed potatoes, scrambled eggs, beacon strips and chocolate chip pancakes.

The breakfast went on quietly for a while and then Michael got up from his chair and addressed everyone. "Okay folks, so this is how it goes. We think we can get you out of here and back to that forest clearing from where Adrian picked you up. I will keep an eye on the forest to track you all leaving from here just to make sure you are not being followed."

Aella looked around curiously. "Wait, that's it? I thought you were going to answer our questions."

Samaar looked at them with concern in his eyes. "For sure. Ask away. I will try my best."

Aella asked again, before Trinity could speak. "What is Sandsmid? Why did Adrian get us here? Who are we running from?" she added throwing a dark look at Adrian, who was pretending quite well to not have heard anything.

Samaar sighed disapprovingly shaking his head at Adrian before turning towards the ladies and answering, "Well Adrian must have thought you guys are being followed and to be honest, we had very few people, living or dead, cross the over into our world. So, it must have alerted the security. Also, this leads us to think of another danger and that is who opened the portal to your world, because that alerted the army for the trespassers. And if you would have been caught alive, you would already have been taken as prisoners. Now, about Sandsmid, let us just say it's like Earth. But a little bit different.

We are not yet sure as to who opened the portal, but we sure do know who is going to come looking for you. Adrian thinks it's best if you guys are just sent to a different location now."

Aella buried her head into her hands while Trinity picked on her teeth. It all got really quiet when Trinity exclaimed, "So if this is really true, and if you guys were not high while telling us this story, I want to mention something that we saw before Adrian hit us."

Aella looked at her questioningly, "You mean to say the footprints?" Trinity nodded. "Adrian, was it you? In the house?" Adrian threw up his hands, "Guilty as charged. I had to wait for you to settle and then come get you. That is the reason I asked to drive alone, I was afraid that something of this sort would happen. But when I got to the forest, I noticed the portal was already open and then I heard your car pull around the front yard. There have been increasing issues with the portals opening more frequently than before. I knew you both got into this place without any knowledge of yours. So, I got out from the back door and the rest you know." He finished looking sheepish.

Samaar got up from his chair. "Enough discussion, we need to get you two out of the portal from somewhere else and get you to another place for a while and lay low. This needs to be done soon before you get tracked." Michael and Adrian silently nodded. Trinity and Aella got up from their chairs to fetch their backpacks.

After a few hours, Trinity, Adrian, Aella and Samaar, all of them got into Aella's car to return.

The rain had toned down to drizzle, but the lightening continued.

Trinity sighed looking at the dark sky outside. The lines by

Haseena that she had read the previous night kept running again and again in her head. 'No one can leave Sandsmid,' she recalled silently shuddering a little.

"So how long have you been in Sandsmid and also managed to be in Toronto with us?" Trinity asked trying to strike up a conversation. She had many questions churning over inside her head, and it was getting tiring at some point for not knowing what was happening.

Adrian smiled. "My orders were to look after you. And, to keep you safe. I was planning to get you here and then to safety, because someone had discovered you back in Toronto by someone from the army who was in disguise. I overheard him informing someone else about you, and I agreed to the plan of our small vacation. You never know who is working for these dangerous people we are going to be at a war with. I felt you will be safer over here for while till we figured out another way, but I am sorry to startle you like that. I felt if I sat to explain you would never understand. Although what still puzzles me is that I was not the one to mess with the portal. It was already open when I got here I and then, I saw you guys all confused and scared."

Trinity watched as they slowly were descending the hill and driving towards the dense thicket they had come from the previous day. However, something felt different. The roads weren't as bumpy as the previous night. Even Aella shuffled a little uneasily. They were going in a different direction. The trees were getting thinner and the roads became more stone clad with a smooth surface to drive on and huge raindrops started pounding against the car windows.

"Adrian, where are we going?" Trinity and Aella asked together. Samaar kept silent and just looked at Adrian, who was tactfully guiding the wheel against the slippery roads. He turned to Trinity just for a split second before answering, "Ladies, just sit tight. I will explain everything soon."

Trinity looked out of the car once again. She stopped and gripped her seat. Adrian drove faster on those roads and soon they reached a cliff. There was a little stone cottage on that cliff. He stopped the car, got out and started walking towards the cliff. It was already a lot of grey clouds swirling around that cliff giving it a dramatic horror look and the cliff itself overlooked a dense forest. The storm was building up again, giving the sky a purple glow. The cottage looked old and dilapidated. There were fresh roses growing around it and the huge front door was half open. All of them got out of the car as well and followed Adrian to the cottage.

They entered. The inside of the cottage was a complete sight. The hall was big and cosy with brown wallpaper lined up all the way till the ceiling. There was a stone wall facing them with hexagon stones around a smoothly carved out fireplace. The windows showed a spectacular view of the valleys. Trinity low-key had started to like this kind of weather. The furniture was all leather and the carpet was a thick rug that looked so much like chinchilla fur.

Adrian calmly sat on the couch and signalled the others to sit facing him. They all sat down, with Aella and Trinity looking at him expectantly. Samaar was mute all this time, letting Adrian take all the limelight.

"Drink, anyone?" he asked offering them a bottle of what looked like some vintage wine. The ladies noticed a mini bar located right behind from where he was seated. He was already helping himself to a glass.

Samaar piped up. "I will have one." Taking a glass from the

bar and pouring himself some wine. Trinity interrupted the dumb charade. "Adrian, Samaar, answers please."

Just as Adrian was about to open his mouth to answer them, they heard loud footsteps. Craning her neck to see who it was, Trinity saw an approaching figure from the distance. A tall woman. She was really talk like six feet and her face looked freckled in a good way. She looked adorable with her mid-length dark green hair. She just stood there staring at Trinity for an eternity, and then her cheeks dimpled as her lips curved into a big warm smile. She looked at Adrian and Samaar excitedly. "Is it her? Is it really her? Does she know? Can I hug her? Holy Siren, she is so pretty. And oh, is this her friend? She looks so sweet and tiny," she said all in one breath jumping up and down like a child.

Trinity took an instant liking to her as compared to Aella who must not have fancied the word 'tiny' a lot. She gave her a tight smile. Adrian and Samaar looked at each other and smiled. "Easy, Brahanne. She doesn't know everything yet, but you sure can hug her."

Brahanne ran at Trinity and smashed herself into her. "Oh my God, I have been waiting for this moment since ages. You are utterly amazing."

Trinity hugged her back warmly. "And so are you, Brahanne. And how do you know about me?"

She pulled back flustered, "Let me introduce myself properly. I do not think these guys would do that for me anyway." She threw a sideways glance at him and continued, "I am Brahanne, the queen of con in Sandsmid. I was told that you exist somewhere, but I did not believe it until I finally saw you. You are our last hope," she said, her smile fading away a little. Looking at Trinity who had an extremely confused expression on her face, she turned to the men in the room yelling, "You tell these ladies everything right NOW."

Adrian lazily put his drink aside. "You're a brat," Aella exclaimed, her hands crossed. Adrian looked at her bemused and answered, "Listen this is all not so easy, I cannot get you back to your original place from where I abducted you both. Trinity you are at a risk of being killed. Aella I am sorry I dragged you into this, you were not at all a part of this plan. I will make sure to help you get out of here safely."

Aella looked at him quizzically, "So why is abducting Trinity so important?" Samaar sighed, "Because she might be able to help us fix Sandsmid."

Trinity felt a lump in her throat, "Why me though? You also mentioned back there that you were sending us both to a different place."

Brahanne at this point put a comforting arm around her. "Why do not you follow me. I want to show you something," she said literally pulling her along with Aella.

She led them through the hallway into a room. The windows were full length and there were paintings on the wall of the same woman that Trinity had seen in her dreams and she bore an eerie resemblance to the women in the paintings back at the 'safe house'. There was a huge jewel studded mirror in the centre of the wall facing her. She also noticed one painting of a dark-haired little baby playing in a gold crib. One painting also included the woman and the baby together. The woman was holding that baby and the baby was reaching out for someone who apparently was not in the frame.

Brahanne and Aella were standing quietly behind her, Aella apparently in her own thoughts, while Brahanne asked Trinity, "You know who that woman in the painting is?"

Trinity was fighting for words, "I do feel like I have seen her before, but I do not know, I am not clearly recollecting, just feel like a lot of things jumbled in my mind right now."

"Well, Trinity, that woman is your mother."

***

In the Desert

Salem was pacing up and down nervously waiting to hear back from Angelica. She must have known about the truth now and she needed to act fast before the time ran out.

The winds howled and rattled the strong glass windows. The messenger should be Angelica herself. She had to be back before the Equinox, so they could start their preparations for the battle they all dreaded.

He looked at the entrance of his dark stone walled trapdoor again. He was glancing there every few minutes wondering what was taking her so long. His worst fears were if she got spotted on her way or killed. He tried his best to bury all those fears inside of him and work on his next move till she came.

Footsteps. They slowly were getting louder. Salem looked up from his work. He expectantly stood up waiting for his daughter to come from that door any moment. The door opened while he rushed towards it and then stopped. The person who was standing there was not his daughter. Anger and fear, both these feelings rushed to his head as he saw had long silver hair and extremely handsome features. "Reh! Where is my daughter."

Reh smiled at him, "Straight to the point always, Salem. You know that is the one quality I loved about you always. You never waste time to ask the right question."

Reh walked around the hall and sat on the chair where Salem had just been sitting. Salem looked at him with anxiety, holding his secret knife clenched tight ready for a fight. "You still didn't answer my question, Reh. Where is my daughter?"

"Oh, she is safe somewhere. For now! She had some really valuable information about the void you know. You need to tell me why you would dare to go against Salvos, Salem. You are aware of the consequences for that."

"I am not going after Salvos alone, Reh. I am going after all of you. The bridge council, so corrupt, we used to have people in Sandsmid before, and now what do we have? Your minions patrolling the levels and some prisoners and the keepers who are your loyal dogs. Where is the world that we should be freely living in?"

"I am impressed. Your fight is for freedom from our rule. I must warn you though, since you already told me your intentions, we as a council are fighting for far more worse thing we fear are coming." There was a glimpse of fear in Reh's eyes that quickly got replaced by his mischievous cunning smile.

With a swift moment, Salem swooped in on Reh with the knife and stabbed him in the arm. Reh, who was expecting the attack shot up from his chair, kicking Salem in the back and pushing him face down. He pulled out his silver sword and thrust it into his knees. Salem let out a cry of agony. He tried to turn over but Reh stood over his body with the sword pushed deeper into his leg. "Enough playing, Salem, tell me what you are up to exactly or we kill your daughter straight away."

"You can kill my daughter all you want, Reh. She will die as a faithful honourable patriot to the real Sandsmid. But you will not be able to beat the storm that is coming for you."

Reh twisted the sword forcing Salem to cry out in pain again. "What storm? Be specific."

Salem snorted. "The storm you had been dreading for years. The battle against the bridges in the presence of Siren? We have a new hero on our side. Salvos's daughter has returned."

5.

Sandsmid: Senge

Trinity stared at her. She had a weird feeling between finding out about something she already knew or discovering something that she had no idea off. All these feelings jumbled up inside her unable to come out. She looked up at the portrait to admire the uncanny similarity to that woman in her dreams. One of the pieces of the puzzle was already fitting in. The clue to her dreams. She turned towards Brahanne.

"My mother? What was her name? You know my parents were ruthless mons..."

"Your foster parents, Trinity," Brahanne finished. "Your parents on Earth. But this lady in the painting, your mother is in Sandsmid, who gave you birth, Dariana, the priestess in the Temple of Siren."

Trinity felt her insides stir. In a way she was relieved to find out she wasn't at all related to those earthly monsters who had not gone a single day without torturing her in some way. But her other side felt she needed to know more about this woman in the painting before she herself came to any kind of conclusion.

"Then why did she leave me? In fact, where is she now?"

Brahanne sighed as if revisiting some old places in her head before answering, "Sandsmid also had people before the council of the bridge came into existence. All the levels that we have, like you have continents were easy to cross and life thrived in the light of the orange sun. Our people worshipped a single goddess called Siren. But then the bridges came…" she stopped to look into the abyss for a minute before continuing, "and changed everything. They started making dark sacrifices in the name of Siren. All the levels were blocked from each other and the people, well some fled who had an idea of the portals, and the rest were taken as prisoners and used as soldiers in the Equinox war that took place a long time ago. Not a lot was left in the aftermath and now the bridge is almost invincible."

Her mother's part had not been mentioned yet. Trinity listened to her patiently. Brahanne spoke again, "And one day you were asked for the royal sacrifice to Siren. Your mother could not bear the thought of giving you up, but she feared the council if she refused. She hid you from them till all these years and she disappeared as well. Adrian got you here when we felt we had enough sources to fight the bridge and we needed you because since Dariana was a priestess, only you can help us find her and the army she has been heard of secretly building against the bridge for all these years."

Leaving Trinity to her own thoughts, Brahanne and Aella who was listening to everything silently walked around the room, giving her some time to clear up her head. Aella came back and held Trinity's hand. "Listen, I am going to be with you in whatever mess you think you are getting yourself in. I just want you not to worry okay?" Trinity smiled at her thankfully. She felt she was blessed to have such an amazing friend.

They moved on to finish the rest of the tour of the house. The house was even grander than she had thought as they went deeper into a maze of hallways and corridors. The gold intricate carvings embellished the walls, and the torches were lit every two metres. The place had four halls, three dining areas, two studies, five bedrooms and a huge library. Trinity was amazed at how much knowledge a library could hold. There were rows and rows of bookshelves laden with books that looked old and new and some looked older than their time. It was fascinating. One of the books even read, 'The Hidden Magics of Siren Temple.' She went to pick it up when her eyes landed on something familiar. 'The Rule of the Bridges'

She put that book aside and took out her own copy from the bag to open the first pages of both the books. Her copy had those lines from Haseena, but the library version of the same book didn't. She hurriedly put her own copy back in her bag and walked on. There were big brass plates covered with strange symbols.

"What are those?"

"The sacred reciting of Siren. It mentions the laws of Sandsmid, who ruled the place in the very beginning, and ways of bringing people back to life."

"You mean dead people,"

"Yes."

They followed Brahanne to a smaller room filled with tons of glowing jewelled antiques. Knives with glowing hilts, anklets and bracelets, ancient jewellery, armour and things Trinity had never seen before. Brahanne fetched something from a nearby table. It was a small round pocket mirror. She handed it to Trinity. "For you, you will need this more than anything. This is more powerful than you think."

"To check you look perfect for every battle," Aella said playfully. Brahanne smiled.

Trinity took it in her hand and observed it. Behind was a

carved image of some woman. There was a tiny hole right in the middle of that carving. Trinity asked Brahanne, "Was this my mother's?" Brahanne smiled and nodded.

They came to the living area where Adrian and Samaar were sitting. Adrian looked at Trinity and Aella who silently nodded at him acknowledging the fact that they had been filled in with all the information required now.

***

In Midland

Angelica struggled against the metal chains. The barricades and the bars told her that she was not getting out of there any sooner. She felt like she had to find a way before those rolls of the information on the levels reached the bridge council.

She looked around her dark cell. There were no probable signs of even the tiniest flaw in it making her, that met her eyes. She guessed she had to be stuck there and inspect the place and think of coming up with the ways to escape so that she could make it to the Equinox sacrifice on time.

She should not have trusted that wretched woman who had tricked her into believing her and got her captured. Hopefully, Salem would have been able to escape whatever she was planning with others. She fumbled around the muddy ground with her hands and started carving with her nails into the mud, everything she was able to remember about the levels that she had read from those rolls. Whatever that description was, if she remembered even some short detail of it, she would be able to use it for her escape.

She thought hard, but nothing popped up in her head. She

sighed. She was probably stuck here till after the Equinox. Trying to fight the tears at her helplessness she closed her eyes and prayed to Siren for hope.

***

Back at Senge

Everyone was pouring over the huge map browsing as Adrian pointed out different places to them. Brahanne and Samaar were aware about everything but it was all new for Trinity and Aella. He was explaining to them about Sandsmid's five levels. The entire world was divided into five levels in a hierarchical manner. The lowest one the Village where only prisoners were kept. The one above it was the Desert. The one after that was Senge in which they were currently. The level up after Senge was Midland, which was consisting of the maximum natural beauty. The final level was the Lighthouse, where the bridge council lived.

Trinity thought of Aella who was standing next to her. Whatever it was, she felt that Aella was being dragged into this unnecessarily. She spoke up, "Adrian, shouldn't Aella be sent back? You did mention back there that you will send us somewhere else? Even if I must stay, I want her to go."

Aella took her hand in hers and said, "No way. If I leave, you leave with me. Or else I stick with you." Trinity looked at her, grateful.

Agreeing, Adrian stood up. "I wish you would stay here, Trinity. I brought you here to show you that you belonged here. But none of us want to force you to fight. You are free to live your normal life. And I apologise for knocking you out earlier. That was the only way I thought of at that time. But I am going to send Aella back safely."

There was a sudden knock on the door. All of them stood there, alert. Adrian signalled something to Brahanne who nodded and pulled Trinity and Aella with her, running deeper into the house.

Trinity heard a loud bang, followed by many footsteps behind them. "Search the place," someone was shouting.

The girls ran after Brahanne and reached that smaller room they had been into earlier. The one with shelves full of glowing jewels. She went towards one of the shelves holding a pocket mirror like the one she had given to Trinity and opened it. She put the open mirror in the middle of one of the shelves and the shelves started moving to reveal a huge dark tunnel. The footsteps from behind them got louder. Brahanne said with an urgency in her voice, "They will not be able to catch me. I know how to escape, but you guys must hurry. Use your mother's mirror, Trinity. You guys stay safe. Go!" Saying this she started taking the mirror from the shelves and the tunnel started closing. Thinking what to do, the girls stood there for a second before entering the closing tunnel, when the footsteps sounded as if they were coming from the room, they were in. "Hurry," Aella urged and Trinity stepped inside first. She turned back to tell Aella to hurry after her and in a split second realised what was going on. Trinity felt Aella's hands reaching out for her for a minute before disappearing. She was captured. The tunnel was almost closed, and Trinity stood right in the centre of that entrance. In no way she could leave Aella. She felt hands reaching out to grab her and Aella screaming, "Trinity, run. Do not worry about me. I trust you. You will find me. Please Go!" The tunnel door snapped when Trinity instinctively stepped back to avoid getting grabbed and fell into darkness.

6.

In the Caves

Shining bees. More like shining pieces of glass. No, it was something else. Maybe a colourful fountain? Trinity squinted in the bright light as she opened her eyes. Trying to adjust to the light and see her surrounding, she slowly tried getting up, but a hand pushed her down. Her head was pounding in her skull, forcing her to remain down.

Moving her eyes, she saw that she was in a cave that had every inch of it covered in mosaic tiles. The tiles formed images of five people. They were in hoods and their faces hidden in the hood's shadow. They were standing in five different places and each had a different coloured background to it.

Faint sounds of a waterfall could be heard faintly, and the air smelled of fresh moisture and wet mud. The walls had more. The mosaic tiles started getting vividly coloured at the base touching the ground. There were tiny line drawings of stick figures running around in those different coloured backgrounds. 'Definitely people fleeing,' Trinity thought. Those five figures appeared ascending from those stick figures. And onto their sides were the same weird symbols she had seen in the library before.

Trinity slowly turned her head to her side. She could feel someone nursing her head with a warm wet cloth. She felt the smooth silk beneath her, and a warm velvet blanket wrapped around her sleeping self. Onto her side were aromatic candles that made the whole scene peaceful and homely. It was a calm feeling and Trinity closed her eyes, relaxed. Just then the last memory of Aella getting caught hit her and she sat up with a jolt.

"Take it easy, kid, you are safe for now."

Trinity turned to look at the woman who just said that. Bright yellow short hair and a short build, she looked back at Trinity curiously as if she were something from a museum.

"But they got my friend, we have to save…" Trinity's voice trailed off as her head started pounding again.

The woman pushed her on her back again. "Rest, kid. You are still weak. I know they got your friend, but you need to recover so you can be strong enough to go save her," she said changing the cloth on her head and replacing it with a warmer one.

Trinity fought back nausea when she tried to speak again, "Who are you? And how did I get here?"

The woman smiled. "Well if you remember falling on your head when you came in through that tunnel. Luckily, I was here, and got you right on time before your skull cracked open. And I will tell you who I am after you take enough sleep."

"So, you knew I was here? How?"

"You need to sleep, kiddo. I promise you will find out soon." And she put her hand on Trinity's forehead who fell into a deep sleep.

***

A man in his late twenties with platinum blond hair and bright blue eyes walked grumpily with the yellow haired woman. They walked quietly for a while, the guy's hand almost getting burned by the low burning of the torch in his hand. He quickly blew it out and pulled another long wood stick from the side of the cave and lit it. He stomped in annoyance.

"Why do you have to give me such stupid tasks? Why cannot someone else do it? And why do you have to be so mysterious? Just tell her your name and be done with it. I have other things to do. You help her out," he said his voice strained.

The woman laughed. "You are too stubborn, you know that? I need to go as soon as I can to rescue Angelica. She thought I was the one who tricked her into going to the Village. I need to be there quick. And you can take care of her. Just do not be too harsh on her okay? She is new and confused. And she just lost her friend." Her brow furrowed with worry. "That is what worries me. The Equinox is coming soon. And that means only one thing."

"Sacrifice," the guy finished, thinking deeply. "But Haseena, how do you know she is ready for all this?" They had been walking in the dark until they reached a clearing. Haseena held the guy back. "You turn back and get her. She is more ready than she knows. Just be nice to her okay?"

The guy nodded. Haseena turned on her heels and walked as fast as she can and soon was well out of his sight. He sighed as he turned back towards the tunnel and started walking in the darkness with the torch wondering whatever he had signed up for was going to change his life or not.

***

Safe House Underground
Adrian treaded steadily trying not to step on the dry leaves in the freezing tunnels. Brahanne was by his side looking smug.

They were halfway over to Midland without anyone noticing but it will not be long before their footprints would be traced. Sandsmid sure was not a great place where technology worked, but tricks? They had plenty.

Brahanne spoke up, breaking the silence, "Shouldn't we have used the same exit that we made Trinity use?"

"That would have been too risky. You know I practically have an invisible radar in my head. They always know where I am. Brahanne, stick close. I think we are nearly there."

They were now walking towards the light that was coming from the end of that tunnel. The walls on either side were become more roughly cut stone paved. It was almost impossible for a regular person to cross the level. There were thousands of mazes of tunnels and that person would be lost in it for the rest of his life. Thankfully, Adrian, who had the experience of all the levels, knew where to go. Brahanne and Adrian looked at each other with an apparent question – "Who will be there on the other side of that tunnel?"

They slowed down their walks to listen to their surrounding and pay attention to any possible risks lurking outside of their cave. Brahanne asked, "How did you manage to get us out of there so quickly before the bridgemen could capture us?"

Adrian looked as if he had been waiting for this question to pop up, "You all never knew that house was right on the edge of the entrance to the Midland maze? I knew there was one more way out of the fireplace, but I had kept that information to myself. Anyway, here we are. You know what to do now. We split up from here."

Brahanne nodded mutely. She had to go far up north, and Adrian had to get Trinity before anyone else got to her. Brahanne knew he would never have let Trinity go down that tunnel on her own if he had the chance, but everything back there happened fast, and they were left with no other choice. She asked the last question, "Adrian, what do you think they will do to Samaar?"

Adrian looked back at her sadly. "I do not know why he wasn't quick enough this time. I am sure he will be fine. I still need time to figure out where they took him. But the only person's life we need to worry about now is Aella's. With the Equinox approaching fast, I think we should hurry. Now go. I need to contact Eddie."

Brahanne pursed her lips and waved a short goodbye before running quickly and disappearing into the thick vegetation outside their tunnel. Adrian watched her go and walked in the opposite direction to look for his friend.

He must have talked for quite a while when he saw two people walking outside a distant tunnel. He crept in the bushes and hid there to listen. Sounded like his friend Eddie. He relaxed and got up, started walking towards the institute. He would meet him there.

***

Trinity opened her eyes. Everything was quiet. She looked around sitting up on her bed. The candles were blown out and that woman was nowhere to be seen. She wondered what time it was. She realised that her headache had completely disappeared, and she felt fresh and energetic. It was hard to make out everything in the distance because of the darkness. She fished around for a match or a lighter in her backpack. She was only able to see her surroundings in the dim light because it came from a distant source somewhere in the cave. Trinity decided to find that source.

Slowly she started walking towards it, bracing herself from her own frightening thoughts. 'What will happen next?' kept circling in her head, but she tried her best to wave it off. Everything was dim and there was not a single soul to be found around her, "Hello, anyone here? Lady with the yellow hair? You there? Someone there?" she called out timidly but all she got in return was her own echoes bouncing off the cave walls. Continuing further, she noticed that the mosaic tiles were everywhere on every inch of the cave surface in strange drawings and paintings that she did not understand. She felt she must have already walked about a kilometre inside her cave now, as she looked back to see just a tiny image of her bed in the distance.

Her surroundings started getting brighter. Now everything was bright and the space she entered was illuminated by a large crystal chandelier and a lot of torches on the walls. She saw that the space was hexagonal. All the six surfaces were covered in mosaic. There were no doors or windows, and the room had no way of exit or entry other than from where she had walked in.

Trinity frantically searched for exit feeling every wall and lying on the floor with ears to the ground to listen to any other kind of noise that denoted a probable exit from this cave. Something caught her eye. It was the painting of the wolves on one of the walls. Five grey wolves looking at her from the wall. One of them however was darker and tinier with a fierce glare. She stared at that painting for a while recalling her dream about the wolves. She was quite sure they were the same ones. 'Trust your heart, do not trust the scene,' they had said.

Her heart racing, she borrowed one of the torches from that

room and walked back to her bed. The dark space slowly lit up and looked much brighter than before. After looking at the wolves she felt a sense of confidence. She was sure they were there to help, no matter if it was in the form of a painting.

While she was pulling on her boots, sitting on the edge of the bed thinking what to do next, she heard the faint sound of the waterfall. The same one she had heard when she woke up for the first time in this cave. That meant the exit was close by. If she could just make out where the sound was coming from. She got up and remembered her mother's mirror. She looked around for it and noticed it was sitting on the table next to the bed along with a letter. She opened it and read,

'You had been unconscious for quite some time. I made a promise to your mother that I would not let anything harm you. I did heal your wounds, but you must get out of this cave. I cannot tell you the exact exit in case you are not Trinity. I have left you a knife that had been my most prized possession till now. It will be handy I assure you. And also, I trust you to find your way out of this cave. You are in a different level now. My trusted source will come to help you. You do not have much time. If this is Trinity, trust your heart and not the scene. Believe in this line and you will be out of here soon. If Siren wishes, we will meet again. Till then, good luck. Haseena'

Trinity held the letter tightly in her hand. So, this was the woman who had written that line in the book. She fished for that book in her backpack and compared the handwriting. Similar. It looked like the woman who had written this letter to her was the same one who had written that line in the book. Also, Trinity felt the similarity between her and those wolves. Something was connected between them. She too had written,

'Trust your heart and not the scene.'

Her heart was inclined towards the sound of the waterfall. She listened closely, and felt it coming from behind the painting of the hooded figures. Behind the mosaic studded wall. It was distant but she could hear it tiny bit louder as she inched closer to that wall.

She started feeling the surfaces, there was a dent somewhere in that wall where she touched. She felt it again. It was in the head of the tallest hooded figure with a red coloured background. She pushed the dent. Nothing happened. She put her hand there again and noticed a tiny stud that looked like a key to a lock hole. She looked around to find something that would fit that stud in its whole. Nada. She even tried to push that stud, but as it was carved out of the wall itself, it did not budge. Time was passing slowly, and she felt hopeless. She reread the letter. 'Trust your heart and not the scene.' Her brain got stuck there. Heart okay. Close to her heart. Her mother's mirror with the dent inside that was almost a tiny hole. Of course. How could she forget the way Brahanne had used the same technique to slide the shelves to reveal that trapdoor?

Without thinking much, she got out that mirror and pushed it onto that stud which fit into that dent perfectly. The mirror turned and the wall turned to reveal a doorknob. Revealed, she pulled the knob and the door creakily opened. She pulled the mirror out of that tiny spot and stuffed it in her pocket. Sliding the backpack over her shoulders, she started walking inside the space that the door had revealed.

She could see a faint black shadow walking towards her. She mentally prepared herself for a fight. For the first time in her life she felt ready. Not a single memory from her past haunted her this time. She slowed down her pace. The shadow was coming closer slowly but steadily. Trinity strained her eyes to look who the person was.

That shadow came close enough for her to know that it was of a guy who looked to be in his late twenties with platinum blond hair and bright blue eyes. He first looked at her bitterly but then nodded approvingly.

"Hello, Trinity, welcome to Midland."

7.

Midland

Trinity stood there looking at him suddenly feeling all exhausted and drained out. That guy studied her for a second before getting aware of his glare making her uneasy.

He extended his hand, "Not to worry. You made it! I am Eddie." Trinity noticed he had a thick heavy accent. "Although I was not at all confident about you making it to here."

'That was indeed not genuinely nice,' Trinity thought, meeting his hand and shaking it. Trinity instantly disliked that dude. His eyes narrowed as he pulled his hand back, "You are still weak. I'm not sure you are ready for what is to come."

Trinity felt her face burn, but she was too tired to snap back. It was strange to feel energetic just a few hours ago and then too much adrenaline felt like it was sucking the life out of her. Or it was because Eddie's presence was making her feel more anxious than she should be feeling. He had a terrible attitude.

He led her in the direction away from where she came from and she started following her quietly. No one made any necessary efforts to make a small talk and she was fine with it. Not even any questions this time. All she wanted to do was to get some sleep and some food. Some delicious food, how good would that be? The sound of the waterfall brought her back to reality. They were close to the exit. She could see the faint light at the end of the tunnel getting brighter and brighter until they were right at the end of it. Eddie made a swift bow saying, "And here is the majestic Midland."

Trinity was in awe at what she was seeing in front of her eyes. It was beyond beautiful. They were on a rocky bank next to which a river with nearly orange looking water flowed. The trees were thick all around the bank and onto their left was that big waterfall, the one that had helped her get out of the cave. It looked surreal as if it was made up of gazillions of tiny crystals. There were dark sandy clouds above them. Although for a change, it was not dark and stormy. The sky had all the sunset hues. And the river that was flowing out of the waterfall had a sunset glow to it. The trees had all dried up dark yellow leaves and the air around them was fragrant with a mild pleasant scent.

"Wow," was all Trinity could manage.

Eddie snorted, "Bet you haven't seen anything like this ever in your life eh? Woods. Right?"

Trinity ignored him. They were now walking on the bank in the direction of that river's flow. The scenery however, remained the same, even if they were walking away from the waterfall, the beauty around was unchanged. They soon reached a huge stone building, that looked very unkempt with bushes and vegetation growing out of every possible window that it had. The entrance had a dark glass door, with a pile of dry branches on the stone steps. She followed Eddie through the door and inside.

Surprisingly, the inside of the building was cosy and once they crossed the threshold, the inside started getting warmer and warmer. The stones walls were well lit and as Trinity followed Eddie to a large room that had a chequered ground, she thought she heard a faint sound of some woman singing. She kept silent and strained to listen, but the sound was too distant to be determined.

That room had a glass chandelier hung low and plush red couches decorated the space. There was a person already seated there. It took a second for Trinity to make out what that person was.

"Adrian?"

"Welcome to Midland, Trinity. I got here as soon as I could. I am sorry about Aella. We are going to get her back."

Tears swelled up in Trinity's eyes. Her only best friend in the world, who had sacrificed herself to save her. She was out there somewhere clinging on to the only hope, that Trinity would get her out of there. She thought about all those moments when Aella was always at her rescue or even if she was having an emotional crisis, she was the only one who had made her feel better. Trinity wiped her eyes and said in a stern voice, "Sure as hell we will. Would you have been able to stop her from getting caught? You or Brahanne?"

Adrian shook his head sadly, "No. I was not even able to save Samaar. I wasn't expecting the raid at all. I am so sorry."

Trinity put a comforting hand on his shoulder. "I am sorry you got into all this mess because of me. I will do my best to help you out. I want my best friend back."

Eddie who had been quite all this time, said rather awkwardly, "Let us all get rest today. We can plan from tomorrow."

Trinity looked around. "What is this place anyway?"

Eddie replied, "The Institute of Oregon. But as you can see, everything has been destroyed."

Adrian sighed, "The bridge."

Trinity nodded. They stood in silence for a while until she

spoke up, "I had one question though. If this is a different world, or dimension, as you guys claim, why do you guys speak the same language?"

Eddie looked at her impressed. Maybe he was not as dumb as he had thought of her to be. He said, "It's because we are aware about your world and languages way more than any of you are about ours. Our languages are ancient and sometimes it becomes extremely difficult to communicate in it. We had many humans here in the past. We can now speak multiple languages of Earth."

Trinity looked at him and nodded. Before she could say anything more, Adrian proposed the idea of food. Wondering how he was going to manage the food, if there were just the three of them, he laughed. "I had arrangements here since we always hide out over here. I had time to set it up before you two came."

The meal was fulfilling. Roasted potatoes and cheese casseroles, just two things on the menu but in a large quantity. Trinity ate to her heart's content in the old rusty dining room with the other two and after dinner, Eddie showed her room.

The room had a huge round bed with silk mattresses. There was a bathroom through the side door and a few paintings on the wall. She saw that all these paintings were plain sandy landscapes. "Sleep, you have a long day ahead of you." Saying this, Eddie left her in the room. Trinity closed the door; she noticed a set of comfortable looking robes on the chair to the side of the room. She changed into them and fell onto the bed. As soon as her head hit the pillows, she was fast asleep.

She woke up in the middle of the night. The faint sound of the singing that she had heard in the morning was coming loud and clear now. It sounded like a woman singing. The voice was mellow, sweet and melodious. However, Trinity was not able to make out the words. She noticed that the sound was coming from outside her window. She walked up to the window and opened it. The sound was now loud enough to be deciphered. But Trinity could not understand the language she was singing in. She looked out. No one. But still the sound came from outside. Suddenly she saw a tiny figure of someone hunched over in the far distance under a tree. Trinity stood there hoping to get a good look at that figure if it came any closer. But the singing abruptly stopped. And then, silence. Thinking she must have been noticed by that figure, she closed the window hurriedly and went back to her bed. She tossed and turned around for a while, till she finally fell into slumber.

She woke up again, this time to the sound of someone knocking on her door. It was Adrian. Dressed in black pants and a blue t-shirt, he looked casual. "You ready? Wake up, lazybones. And get fresh. There is an entire wardrobe there for you," he said pointing at the wardrobe behind her. Trinity had noticed it the previous day, where it stood there looking useless in the far corner of the room. She went inside and opened it. It was stacked with all kinds of different outfits. Normal, strange, weird and for some strange reason, long silk robes. She tried to find something that was comfortable and functional. She finally slipped into a pair of trousers with a white tank and a green cardigan. She went down feeling fresh and thinking when was the last time that she had a proper shower. Adrian and Eddie were already seated in the dining area when she arrived. The table was laden with food. Trays of apples, fresh bread, boiled eggs, roasted potatoes, rice and yogurt. She sat down and joined them.

Eddie pulled out a book, looking ready to take down notes,

"Okay so how do we do this?"

Adrian looked up, "Do what?"

"We have to figure out a way to cross this level, so we can reach the Lighthouse."

"Cross Midland? Shouldn't we be saving Aella first?"

"That is where she is kept. The Lighthouse."

Trinity felt a chill down her spine. Why were they so sure about where she was kept? "How are you so sure? What are they going to do to her?"

"I am not sure but… You tell her Adrian." Eddie said, agitated, unable to bring out the next words.

Adrian took a deep breath. "They won't do anything to her until Equinox. Then I am not so sure."

"Sure about?"

Adrian expertly avoided that question. "We have to find one woman to help us cross this level, Eddie. You know she is the best person who will help us cross this level."

"Speaking about a woman, did you two hear someone signing last night?" Eddie and Adrian looked at her, confused. "Who was signing? What woman?"

"Do not pretend. It was loud and obvious. When I looked in her direction, I felt as if she must have noticed me and stopped."

Adrian got up. "Well, I do not know what woman you are talking about, but if she noticed you, we need to move from here fast. Get your backpack and meet me here."

They all dispersed. Soon everyone was down and walking out of the institute from the back of the building. It was denser and thicker than the front yard. Struggling to keep up with the guys, Trinity asked Adrian, "Where are we going?"

"We are going to get someone who knows this level better than any of us. But she will not talk to us, because of umm an incident that deterred our friendship in the past. We want you to convince her to help us."

"Adrian what are they going to do to my best friend?"

Adrian replied anxiously, "Trinity I am not sure but what likely happens when someone is taken a prisoner in the Lighthouse is a sacrifice."

Trinity stopped dead in her tracks, Eddie and Adrian slowed down to give her some space. "Trinity, we are sorry. We will try our best to get her back."

"Try your best? I am going to GET her back. No trying. Let us go."

And then it was less talking and more walking. Trinity noticed they were walking even farther away from the direction of the waterfall. The trees started getting sparse. There was more of a clearing ahead and she noticed that there were hills that resembled waves frozen midway. They almost touched the clouds. The dark clouds also thinned a little, letting the sunset sky spread its shades making everything look multicoloured. There were round trees everywhere of bold colour and very few empty looking houses dispersed around that area.

Trinity noticed that the trees were brighter and had more than one colour than the ones she had seen near the waterfall. Orange and maroon were the new additions. The whole scene looked magnificent. She had never seen anything that was this beautiful, that it even made the waterfall's shine fade a little. She stopped taking in the view as much as she could.

Adrian and Eddie stopped as well. Adrian put his arm around Trinity and pointed her to the nearest cottage. It was an old lightwood structure barely managing to stand on its own. "This is where she lives. Sahara! If we go in there with you, she is never going to understand the seriousness of this matter. But if you go in there first and tell her who you are, she might believe you."

"Okay. Doesn't sound that bad."

Adrian nodded. Trinity walked over to the cottage alone. The front door had a small landscape painting on it. Sandy landscape. She gently knocked on the door. Someone from inside said, "It's already open. Come in."

Trinity pushed the door and it squeaked as it swung open. She went inside to a large empty space. The walls were solid light sand coloured and the floor had an ochre coloured carpet spread out over it. There was no one there. She called out loudly. "Hello?"

A petite figure emerged from behind one of the walls. Trinity saw that she was a thin short woman with long chestnut coloured hair reaching her waist, and she had tiny green eyes and a mousy little face. According to Trinity, she looked like a pixie. She was staring at Trinity intently. Then to her amusement, she looked down, shook her head and sighed.

"Tell me, girl, did Adrian send you here?"

***

In the Desert

An injured Salem lay on the floor, with his own blood around him. He had been trying since the past few hours to get up, but in vain. Reh had spared his life, leaving him wounded in his house. He had vanished through that trapdoor immediately after hearing about the news of the daughter of Salvos.

Shifting the weight to his both arms, he started pushing hard on the ground. Slowly he managed to sit up. With the help of his hands, he crawled a bit towards the wall so he can lean against it. He pulled out the fabric belt from his cloak and painfully looked at his leg. The sword was still deep into his leg. But that did control the bleeding up to an extent. He put one hand around the sword and started pulling it with all his might. He tried to control his screams through his gritted teeth, slowly and stealthily pulling the weapon out of his almost dead leg.

As he was about to pull it out completely, he heard the footsteps from the trapdoor again. Snuffling painfully, he pulled the sword out and quickly with shaking hands tied the belt tightly around the wound. He took the sword in one hand and, still leaning against the wall, panting, waited for whoever it was coming to appear in front of him.

An average tall woman with long black hair, wearing black pants and a red flare blouse rushed towards him and knelt next to him, examining his leg. "The wound is deep but not deadly. You will be okay in a few days. I am here to help you. We need to find your daughter soon. Salvos is not going to stop. And the more we spend our time doing nothing, the stronger him and his army are going to get. Salem, tell me what I should do to make the healing faster. For those who have fought wars for years, such wounds take no time in vanishing."

Salem, still in shock of everything that was happening, snapped back into his senses and directed her, "All the essential oils for such injuries and gauze tapes are in the chest in my room. It is in the west of the trapdoor you just came from." The woman got up to fetch all those things, when he stopped her, holding her hand and looking at her questioningly,

"Dariana, tell me the real reason why you came out of your hiding."

8.

Midland

Trinity was about to reply when Sahara started yelling at her.

"Get out! I am not falling for any tricks by Adrian this time."

"Sahara, I am Trinity. I am…"

"I do not care whoever you are. I am not standing for any of his gimmicks. He nearly got me dead once. Not this time. Get out!" She was shaking. Trinity just stood there wondering how strongly this pixie was lashing out.

Trinity held up her hand. Sahara, still shaking looked at her curiously. "I am Dariana's daughter."

She stopped for a second but then got her angry expression back. "Prove it," she said, crossing her arms like a stubborn child.

Trinity seeing no point in arguing any further, got out her mother's mirror from her backpack and tossed it at Sahara. She caught it in her hand and examined it.

"Oh, it is really you. Sure you have not stolen it from someone else right? How do I not know that you are a con artist who stole Dariana's mirror?"

"You do not. You will only find out the truth if you be patient enough," Trinity said standing there calmly. She was witnessing the change in her own behaviour after finding out that she had someone she could call a 'family' in Sandsmid.

Instead of a constantly apologising and confused Trinity who was always haunted by her past, she was feeling herself to be a confident and brave woman.

Sahara looked at her. She too must have noticed the authenticity in Trinity's voice. She closed her eyes, took a deep breath and opened them to frown at her. "I know Adrian must be around here somewhere. That moron always needs my help for something or the other, but he never ever helps me. Very well, call him in."

Trinity smiled at Sahara's accuracy at predicting Adrian's nature. She said, "Well we have one more addition to our little group. Eddie. I do not know much about him, but he seems okay."

Sahara laughed. Trinity was relieved to see Sahara in a normal mode. She said, "Mark my words, Trinity. When the time comes, Eddie can be trusted more than Adrian. Now call them in and let us hear what those two have to say."

Trinity went out and called the two guys waiting outside. They were just standing there like motionless bodyguards not even looking at each other, completely stiff. "Oy, Sahara wants to talk," Trinity called at them. They both sprang into motion and trotted towards the house. Sahara gave a half-hearted hug to each of them.

"So, Adrian, what do you guys want from me?"

"We want you. No one else knows how to cross this level and reach Lighthouse."

"Okay. I knew if this was Adrian's idea it was not going to be an easy thing. What do I get in return?"

Adrian looked at her uneasily. Eddie spoke, "You enjoy making Adrian uneasy. Well, what do you want?"

Sahara replied with a twinkle in her eye. "If I get you past the Keeper Village and till the border, I get the institute."

Adrian looked at her doubtfully. "You mean the Institute of Oregon? What are you going to do with it?"

"None of your business. I know you are in the ownership of that place. Consider it as a payback for how you got me in trouble last time. If not, then you all can leave."

Eddie held up his hands. "Done. Now help us, Sahara. Trinity's friend is in trouble. She is not from Sandsmid. She doesn't have much time."

Concern spread across Sahara's face. "I will try my best to get you guys across. But be warned. This level, as beautiful it looks, is equally dangerous. Follow me."

Sahara ushered all of them into the door near the hallway that had steps which descended into a basement. The basement was all dark, but even then, Trinity could make out the sandy patches of colour here and there on the walls and the floor. She closed the door behind them, and all huddled in a dark corner of the basement. The rustling of the leaves could be heard from outside and then sharp squeak of the front door. Sahara perked up alert. "I think you have been traced. We need to hurry." Sahara knelt trying to move the carpet over which they had been standing. Someone during this process stepped over Trinity's foot. "Ouch." "Sorry," she heard Eddie say from her side.

Sahara's voice came from a little farther, "Guys, let us go, hurry." The carpet was indeed covering up a set of stairs. They climbed down another dimly lit flight of stairs into a dingy small room. Its walls were covered with the same strange symbols, Trinity had seen before. Right in front of her was a glass cubicle. Right in the middle of that small room. Looked useless to her. It was not as if someone secretly came down to take showers in here, not that it had any faucets or anything. It was just a glass cubicle. A closed space.

Sahara's face was filled with disdain as she opened the door to the cubicle. Trinity asked concerned, "What is it Sahara?"

She shrugged and looked at her. "Just travel jitters. Stay safe Trinity. And all of you. Our trails are being traced and if we do not take action soon, we might go down the same way as all the others who have tried to defy the bridge have gone."

Trinity spoke her wisdom for the first time, "Sahara, I have been running from them since my day one in Sandsmid, and I do not even know what I have done wrong. I might even be on the wrong side by supporting all of you. But what I have felt in all these days is, whether you like or not, just stay one step ahead. It always gives us time to think about the consequences for the right or wrong that we do."

Sahara smiled at her proudly. "You have your mother's genes. I hear you. We should get prepared right away. This area has been designed to keep the army of the radar. We will split into two groups. I will leave with Adrian and you go with Eddie. Also, I might add something. Trinity do you know anything about our ancient language. Eddie should start teaching you some of it when you reach. The symbols you see around here are in that language. If you truly belong to Sandsmid, you will not take long to learn it. It is going to be in your blood. Now, I got distracted. Back to instructions. You and Eddie start walking south towards the lake. I and Adrian will meet you by the lake. This level is tricky. Try not to get distracted by anything, because if you do, you will spend your three lives there and still won't be able to cross."

Trinity got annoyed by that. "What is with these levels?

Why does everyone exaggerate so much about them being so difficult to cross? You all did anyway, right?"

Sahara answered, "No. I just know how to get past this level. I never have myself. I have spent my entire life in Midland and so has Eddie. Only Adrian has been around everywhere. And that is why I do not trust him." She cast him a dark look.

"I have a history with conning people. That is how I and Brahanne learned to cross the levels with a bunch of other experienced people and we grew up doing it," Adrian replied.

"Then why do we need Sahara for this level?"

"Because a lot has changed since the last time I had been in this level. We do not know now who have switched their sides and might snitch on us," Adrian said.

"Sounds fair," Trinity said. She hugged herself before saying, "Guys! Let us do this. It is going to be okay. For Aella."

"And for Sandsmid. And, for Samaar!" the others chimed in.

Eddie spoke up, "So, I shall make the first move and Trinity, you follow me. This glass cubicle is like a teleportation funnel. And it has been designed to take you only to one place. Trinity, if you do not see me when you land, just keep walking south of where you have landed. Do not stop, do not answer to anyone on the way until you see me. This is if we both do not end up in the exact same place. Sometimes this guy does that," he said pointing at the cubicle.

Trinity nodded. "So, this is how you go from one place to another. By travelling at the speed of light. If Sandsmid is this advanced, why can't you defeat the bridge?"

"Because they are more advanced than we are," Adrian said the obvious. "Plus, they have weird rituals for sacrifices."

Trinity shivered at the last word. She thought about Aella and then got herself together. She was going to save her. And she was going to do it even if that meant risking her own life. She looked at Eddie who got into the cubicle and closed the door. He smiled at her. Trinity was about to say 'travel safe' when Sahara nudged her from the back.

"I trust you would be able to make it out of this level, Trinity. I have faith in you, whether you are an impostor or not. Just try and remember how you got into Midland and it would be useful for you when you reach the lake."

Trinity looked back to see that Eddie had already vanished. She lowered her voice and answered, "I do not really know how I managed to get out, Sahara. I guess I got a lot of hints from a woman called Haseena. She was the one who nursed me. Anyway, now my turn," she added stepping into the glass cubicle.

Sahara looked quizzical and walked quickly to Trinity before she could close the door and whispered, "Haseena, you said? It was rumoured that she was killed the night you disappeared from Sandsmid."

Saying this she pressed the door of the cubicle tight shut and everything in front of Trinity started blurring and vanished the very next minute.

***

Lighthouse

Aella opened her eyes. She still felt sedated. It must have been days being unconscious she realised as the last thing she remembered was the hands grabbing her and the next thing she knew was darkness.

She laid on her back across the cold hard floor. She felt giddy and cold. Cold as in feverish cold. Her eyes darted around to figure out where she was. It was a circular room. Dark. Faint light came from the window above her. It was the light from outside. Bright blue sky. She tried to clutch the wall behind her, her fingernails scratching the wall. She winced as that pain seared through her fingertips. Trying to keep balance she finally managed to crouch, with her head still resting against the wall. She could see above her that the window had no bars. If she could just escape from the window. She tried to get up and touched the carving of the stones.

With great efforts she got up and steadied herself. Eagerly she cast her glance at the window with hopes, but it wasn't long before all her hopes sunk. The view outside showed that she was on top of a tall tower around that area because when she looked down, she saw endless darkness. She jerked back and fell to the ground. Putting her head between her legs, she tried to take a deep breath, pushing back her tears. She knew Trinity was coming for her. She had faith in her. Meanwhile she decided she was not going to sit there like a damsel in distress. She decided she would try to figure a way out of this mess. She knew she was a prisoner somewhere, but she had to know for what. Was she going to be killed or used as a bait? She had to find that out.

She began scanned the room. There was water kept at the other end and some cold food. She grabbed the food and chowed it down. Immediately she felt better. There were no possible exits except the large wooden door that was locked. If she tried to jump out of that window she would fall and break into a thousand pieces. Controlling her panic, she started thinking of ways she could draw someone's attention to her. She heard someone talking outside her door. The door was old and huge but the slot from which they slid food to the prisoners had no flap. She knelt to down to listen to the conversation. Sounded like two men were talking about an important event.

"Watch over her. We cannot afford to lose her. She is precious to us."

Aella felt they must be talking about her. She strained her ears to listen more.

"Salvos was furious the time his daughter was kidnapped. Not this time. She is perfect for Siren. She will be the great sacrifice for Equinox. Thank Siren, she is going to be in slumber for long enough to not find out about all this."

Aella swallowed. So, she did not have much time. She was well, going to be sacrificed as they said. She prayed for Trinity to hurry. She was trying her best to be strong when she heard them say, "Our prisoner doesn't know she is friends with the daughter of the leader of the bridge. Look where it got her."

9.

Midland Border

Trinity hit her head with a thud against the glass. "Ouch," she cried. Everything appeared foggy and slowly started coming into the focus of her vision. She felt dizzy from her little teleportation 'trip'. She got out of the glass cubicle and found herself being hit in the face by blasts of cold air. She looked around. Goosebumps crawled on her skin and the cold made her want to go back to the cubicle and shut the glass the door. She was out in the open and there was no one around. Not even Eddie. And nothing to be seen around. No trees, no forests no beautiful waterfalls like the one she had seen back then. The area looked dead and deprived of any kind of vegetation and the place gave off a very dry vibe that filled her with dread. The first the thing that came into her mind was to get out of there.

She started walking ahead opposite the direction of the cubicle. It was so strange to see a glass cubicle in the middle of nowhere. Totally made sense, no one was going to suspect anything. She had to look for Eddie. But if she stayed back and waited, she would probably freeze to death. Her outfit didn't provide the luxury to keep herself warm. She pulled out another cardigan from her backpack that would help her get stable, and the walk was keeping her muscles worked up, so she stayed a little warm. Dry lifeless land everywhere till her eyes could see. And no one in sight. Trinity started walking faster and then almost broke into a sprint. The lifelessness of the place appeared foreboding. The same landscape and the same skies. If it had not been the glass cubicle left behind, she would have felt that she was stuck in the same place going in circles. But she knew that she was leaving the place from where she had come far behind.

Her hope hanging on loose ends, she called out in panic. "Eddie? Adrian? Sahara? Where are you guys? EDDIEEEEE!" She yelled her lungs out but no answer. She gave it one more shot. "Eddie? Are you here? Please reply. I am here." No answer. The yelling was all in vain.

Spending every ounce of the energy she had left; she ran as fast as she could blindly ahead and collapsed exhausted on the ground.

The air shifted and she felt a warm whiff on her face before feeling the same cold air again. She lay loose on the ground, dirt getting on her clothes and hair. She closed her eyes, fighting the panic down her throat. It was not how she expected her life to end. No one was going to even know what had happened to her. But even amidst the still skies and the lifeless grounds, she managed a smile hugging herself tightly to keep warm. She thought of how her life had taken a turn, and she meant something to someone. Not the abusive foster parents, not the rude classmates from school, but real friends who did everything to keep her safe and a place that gave her purpose. Maybe if she died here due to hypothermia or starvation, one part of her was okay to let go, because of how she had felt these past few days. Her eyes were closing. Exhaustion and dizziness were taking over her consciousness. The last thing she remembered before she finally gave in to an exhausted sleep was seeing a woman singing in a melodious song in a language she could not understand.

***

Beads of sweat broke over Eddie's forehead as he called out for Trinity again. It had been quite a while since he had arrived through the glass cubicle but oddly enough, the landscape was different. When he got out of the glass cubicle, he was surrounded by a thicket of dry trees. He knew where he was, and he knew that one of the side effects of this glass cubicle was its multiple locations around the borders of Midland. But he was not worried about his location. What made him nervous was that there was still no sign of Trinity anywhere. He was worried if anything happened back there before she could travel, or was she stuck somewhere trying hard to get out of there. Hope she followed the rules of not stopping and not talking to anyone, because the borders were filled with snitches who sided with the bridge who must have probably placed a bounty over Trinity by now.

Eddie started walking admiring the ancient stone ruins around him. Monoliths with symbols carved in on them loomed over him, as if protecting him from the unknown. Eddie walked, his feet making scrunching noises against the dry grass. In front of him was a huge ruin, with weeds growing through it. The ruin looked deserted, but Eddie could sense movement behind the large stones that were almost blocking the entrance. He climbed onto a niche of one of the stones and got past them and entered the ruin.

Just like a predator who had been waiting for his prey, someone leaped on him from the back and knocked him down with a strong punch. But Eddie had been prepared for this. He immediately leaped up and blocked the next punch from the person who was much taller than him, with beady eyes, shiny skin and long hair braided behind his back. That person looked at him and shouted in a strange language. Eddie grabbed his throat, backing him off and held him there with his leg on his chest. The stranger narrowed his eyes, ready to throw his spear at him when Eddie shouted, "Kryptal, I know you. I need your help."

The stranger stopped. Still on his alert, and spear in position, he asked, "How do you know me? If you are one of the keeper's pets doing their dirty work for them, I swear on Siren, you are not going to get out of here alive." His eyes twinkled when he said the last sentence.

"I am not here to do keeper's work. I want you to help a friend. Sahara had mentioned you ages ago. I knew you are not with them. But I am worried someone else might be in trouble if they find her out."

The guy eyed him suspiciously. "What friend?"

"Her name is Trinity. The daughter of Dariana. We must help her. I fear she must have landed into the 'hollows fields' and she is going to be lost there."

"Did you say Dariana?"

Eddie nodded silently. Kryptal backed off, putting his spear down and sat on the ground. His next words were filled with worry. "I hope she is still there."

"Of course she will be. How far are the fields from here? Can we get going right away?"

Kryptal got up. "Anything for Dariana's daughter. Let us go. I know a way to get there quickly. Follow me."

They walked past the ruins and into the thicket. But instead of a clearing, the trees grew dense. Eddie asked, "What way is this?" "It's from the back of the forest. So, we will reach there fast. Ah, here we are, in no time."

They ran out in the clearing and into the fields. No one in sight. They looked around for a while. Eddie tried calling out to Trinity several times. But no answer. Something glistened in the far end of the field. Eddie noticed it and pointed it out to Kryptal. They reached there to see a tiny metal amulet, reflecting in the dusk light. Kryptal picked it up. "Oh no. I hope Trinity is safe."

Eddie looked at his worried face in surprise. "Why, what is it?"

"The keepers have her."

***

Temple Tales

A lot of bells were jingling. The sound was sweet to the ears. Trinity felt her eyelids were heavy. Was that how someone felt when they died? She thought she would be able to see some divine lights but there was just darkness. What purgatory was she stuck in. She tried to move but her limbs were too stiff. She tried to open her eyes again. She had fancied the art of passing out since she had come to Sandsmid, she thought to herself bitterly. But the good news was, she was not dead after all. Her eyes slowly adjusted to the dimly lit surrounding. She was in a chamber. The stone walls were no more a surprise for her. But the green torches were. She had never seen green flames before. There was a man and a woman looking down at her. They had strange appearances. Both had long braided hair and were unusually tall. The woman was wearing a long cloak that appeared rugged and a lot of amulets and chains jingled on her neck when she moved. The man was bare chested with just rugged pants and a sinister expression in his eyes.

Trinity struggled to sit up. The man and woman did nothing to help. They just kept watching her. She sat up straight and rested her back against the bed rest. "Who are you? Why do you have me here?"

The man spoke, "You were in our lands. We should ask you the same."

Trinity held her hand up to her head. She felt warm in those green flames. "I am Trinity. From another world. I need to reach the lake. I am not here for any trouble."

The man straightened up. His expression getting warm. The woman still appeared stiff. He spoke, "So you are a child who accidently got lost in the 'Willow fields'. I can understand that. It is easy to get lost into those fields. An extremely unfair creation of nature in here I suppose. Why do you need to go to the lake may I ask?"

Trinity had just met these people. Trusting them was out of question. Telling them her name seemed an overshare enough. She answered, "Meeting some important people there."

"Then you need good rest. You had given up by the time we reached you. I saw you walking in the middle of those fields and decided to bring you here. We knew you were weak enough to fight us, so we kept you in our chamber in case you proved to be a threat. But it looks like you are not. I am Zen and this is my wife Zella. We are the keepers. And we look after the 'Temple of Siren'," he said, pointing at the woman.

Well Zella for sure looks like a threat, Trinity thought. Sensing her uneasiness, Zen said again, "We will send some food over here. Rest up and then depart on your journey whenever you feel you are strong enough." Saying this he and Zella left the chamber.

Trinity got out of her hard bed and walked around. The dark grey stone had a smooth surface. The chamber had a narrowly inclined ceiling, with an unevenly elliptical opening to see the outside. Trinity looked outside. The sky was the same as she had seen before she had passed out. But instead of fields, there were just trees. Trees with yellow leaves. It was big enough for her to climb out. But to where? She might as well look around for a while before she can escape. The chamber was empty except for the bed she had been passed out on and those weirdly green torches and her backpack in the corner. She checked it and let out a relieved breath. No one had gone through it. The book and the mirror and the knife, everything was still there. Maybe these people could be trusted. But she still wanted to prepare herself for the worst. Running out after getting some food felt like a good idea.

Just then, the aroma of something delicious wafted through the air. Simple potatoes and weird looking fruits. Zella got in a leaf with this food and set it at the foot of Trinity's bed. Giving her a steely look, she left without saying a word. Trinity saw the food and the next thing she knew was the terrible hunger that made her realise she had not eaten anything for long. She gobbled it down hungrily. Soon, she felt full and sleepy. Trinity thought she could escape from the opening after she woke up. Her head getting heavy suddenly, she drifted off into peaceful sleep.

Not long after, she was woken up by the sound of wolves howling outside. She sat up to find Zen and Zella staring at her again. "Guys, you have to stop doing that. It creeps me out," Trinity cried out in frustration. She started to stand up when something felt heavy on her legs. She looked there and realised her legs were in shackles. Heavy metal shackles, impossible to break. Trinity looked at the couple angrily. "I knew you were scheming shmucks. You drugged my food didn't you?"

Zen smiled. "Well you shouldn't have eaten it then. And you told us your name. You know there is a bounty over it? You would like to know that we are loyal to the bridge council. Sorry, child," Zen said with a little regret in his eyes.

Zella scoffed. Trinity for sure detested this wretched woman. Zella looked at her sharply and said, "I am not sorry. You came into our lands. We did not ask you to. I bet our prisoners could use some company."

Saying this, they left. There was no door from where they had come. But there was no way Trinity could break those chains and escape. She felt foolish for trusting the strangers. But where were her friends? No one showed up. She could have easily escaped through the opening if she wouldn't have waited for the food. But then, who knew what was waiting there outside for her. She needed to think smart to break those chains. Trinity tried reaching out for her bag, but it was too far. The shackles in her legs were tied at the edge of the bed and not long enough for her to get up and walk around her bed. She sighed. Maybe she could try breaking the wooden frame of the bed. She started knocking her chained leg against the wooden frame. It made a racket, but she did not care. She had to get out.

Suddenly she saw another person climbing into her room from that opening. He had a similar look to Zen but was more strongly built. He had sandy brown eyes. Terrified, Trinity opened her mouth to scream, but the man put a finger on his lips pleadingly.

"Trinity, I have come to rescue you. Stop making noise. We

do not have much time."

Trinity looked at him. "How do I trust you? Two of your kind just sold me to a cult council."

The man replied, "Because Eddie sent me to get you."

***

Angelica woke up groggily. She was still on the ground of her dark prison cell. But the noise that had woken her up was coming from outside. A woman was screaming. And then all was quiet. Angelica huddled further back into her cell. She knew what was happening. Another prisoner was going to be added in her prison. Soon sounds of chains dragging on the ground was heard. It was not long before she would have to witness the pity sight of another helpless prisoner being dragged into this dark cell soon to be handed over to the council. It was only a matter of time before their soldiers came for her as well.

She closed her eyes, the tears stinging. There had to be some way to end this monstrosity. The keepers were getting ruthless. Suddenly she heard a melodious tune. She looked around. Someone was singing a song in an extremely sweet soothing voice. The source of sound was coming from the inside of the cell and it appeared to be a woman's voice. But she could not see anything in the dark. She tried to listen calmly to the song and sat there dazed hearing the words,

"Sister, sister hear me out,
The winds gave away and the storm got loud,
Maiden, we crouched beneath,
They snatched our hopes and burned our tree,
Searched for treasures in the rocks underneath,
And bound those souls who once roamed free,

What blood stays calm,
In the ruin they wept in pain,
The silver sword sliced my palm,
Rise, rise, the war they fought in vain,
Take back our willow lands,
Take back our gods,
Mother, she holds out her hands,
The armour shone off odds,
Heed to my warnings, heed to my shout,
Sister, sister hear me out!"

Angelica snapped out of her trance. The song was sweet and soothing. But her heart started beating rapidly. She had to find her way out fast, for she knew what the song meant. The song was a war cry.

10.

Temple of Siren

Trinity looked at him with her arms crossed. "Who are you?"

The man sighed. "I am Kryptal, Eddie's friend. Actually, Sahara's. I had rescued her back when she was lost once. Eddie and I went looking for you in the hollow fields, but you were already gone. And we found an amulet that led me to you here. I knew the keepers would love to seize every chance they would get to sell anyone that crossed their lands."

Trinity was uncertain. Anyone can make promising statements to convince her. And she didn't know much about these strange lands anyway. Kryptal ignored her expression and looked at her chained legs. The shackles were thick. He took his spear and started brushing it against them, which made loud screeching noises. Trinity looked at him blankly. "You just asked me to stop making noise."

"But my spear can cut across this metal quickly. What you were doing was painful to hear."

"And this is music to my ears," Trinity said rolling her eyes.

But Kryptal for sure was fast enough. Soon Trinity's legs were free of those heavy chains and she leaped to her feet and grabbed her backpack. Once again, she checked it. Everything was in there. She and Kryptal climbed out from that opening in the chamber.

The moment Trinity's feet landed on the ground; she nearly fell into the contoured dry grass. She saw that there were contours on the land they were standing in, as if fields carved into steep steps leading up to a domino-looking monolith in the centre of that land.

Trinity looked at Kryptal and asked, "What is all this?"

Kryptal spat bitterly, "Sacrificial place. We need to get out of here as soon as possible. The guards must be alerted by your disappearance."

"Speaking of which, how come they did not keep tight security or were alerted by the noises?"

Kryptal smiled. "Because you are new to this place. And they know that. So, they will be carefree about the fact that you will even try to run away. And if you do, without anyone's help you will again get stuck in the hollow fields and they could retrieve you from there. Anyway, there's Eddie."

Trinity looked at where he was pointing. Eddie was walking towards them, all dusty and exhausted. He eyed Trinity with concern and then glared at her.

"What? It's no fault of mine." Trinity said defensively.

"You do have a knack for finding troubles, do you not?"

Trinity made a face and crossed her arms. "Well, you do have a knack of not giving any proper instructions as to what will happen if I land somewhere I wasn't supposed to."

Eddie looked as if was about to argue but then shut his mouth looking elsewhere.

"We need to walk fast. We will be outnumbered by the keepers if we stay here for long."

Everyone agreed. They hurriedly walked past the sacrificial grounds and into the thicket. The walk was short and exhausting with their feet crushing the dry grass on the ground. Trinity hugged herself again, trying to keep warm from the cool air while Eddie trotted a little behind.

"Eddie, what are the hollow fields?"

"They are big pieces of dry lands. The keeper's village is under a fog that reflects the light and makes these fields look endless. I figured you must have walked almost to their village but collapsed right outside."

"Speaking of, who are these keepers?"

Kryptal spoke up, "Priests. They are the only ones who have the access to all the rituals performed to appease our holy Goddess Siren. These rituals contain ceremonies, sacrifices and calling upon dark energies. Years ago, this wasn't the tradition. People were at peace. Siren was just worshipped with flowers and prayers. The priests at that time recited the ancient prayers from our sacred rolls and everyone was happy. But then," he sighed.

Trinity urged, "But then?"

"But then, the bridge council came into existence and everything changed. At first, they accepted the localities and traditions. Then slowly started mixing their malicious intent into their acceptance. Slowly it got so corrupted that a living being was sacrificed every Equinox to Siren."

Chills spread in her blood and Trinity knew they were not because of the cold air. She wanted to know more. "But you are one of them, right? What made you cut loose?"

"I was. But then I saw innocent people being sacrificed for magic and power and short-lived riches. The kind that should upset Siren. I do not want to believe in a god that consumes countless innocent souls. I tried to stop them, but Zen, the leader of the village now, asked me to leave in peace and never show my face again. I became an outcast, and he turned my people against me. I went into the ruins to live a life of my own. I still have my ancient rolls with me, so I study them, they keep me company."

"Yes, that ghastly Zen. I wish I could light his braid on fire. And who is this god you all keep on worshipping? Siren?"

"She is our only god. Or goddess, whichever you prefer. She was born out of a red star and came to these lands to share some life. In her story, that we have in our scriptures, she is the goddess of war. She prayed for the bread and worked for the water. The lands got soon blessed with the lakes and rivers and beautiful mountains and valleys. But this land has a red sun. And it lies below the sands of your Earth and above the depths of the void. That is how our world was called Sandsmid."

"But why is she a goddess of war?" Trinity asked again. All this information was overwhelming for her. She noticed large rocks starting to appear here and there with large stone structures in the far distance ahead. Her feet had begun to ache, but she hardly noticed, caving in for more information.

"The sacred scrolls mention her giving a war cry when things were dire. Her job was to restore the peace and end the conflicts between the Sandsmid people. She would walk bare footed, with her flute singing out to those helpless hiding in their homes to come out and fight for justice. And those who heard her would get the strength to fight. In the scrolls it is also written that she used to lead the armies against the human invaders. Before the bridge council was formed, a war was fought where all five levels waged battle against those invaders. Not much was left in the aftermath, and our people lost all hope. Siren just became a symbolic goddess after that, and our people chose other people to lead and govern them and thus was born the bridge council."

"So that's it? She just went 'poof' after the war? Honestly, goddesses do not do that and by the way, you mentioned she was born out of a star. So that makes her an alien," Trinity said as a matter of fact.

Kryptal looked at her with disbelief. "You just insulted our god."

"I am not insulting. Just stating a fact. And so according to what you said, the magic by those keepers is making those fields look infinite?"

Kryptal nodded. Eddie had been listening to this conversation silently. It appeared he too was interested in the talks about the ancient times.

They had almost reached the big ruin, with three huge stones at the entrance. Kryptal easily pushed the first stone to the side to make way for them to pass. Eddie looked at him bemused. "Really? And you couldn't do that for me? I had to climb over these stones to get to you."

Kryptal shook his head smiling. Trinity had a few more questions, she wanted to ask. She opened her mouth but Kryptal held up his hand to silence her for a minute and said, "Welcome people. This is my humble home. Now, Trinity, you can ask."

"Thank you, Kryptal for letting us crash here," Trinity said thankfully, entering the stone ruins and inside the open chamber instantly feeling warm.

"Crash? What are you crashing?" he asked, alarmed.

Trinity waved her hand away playfully. "Oh, that was just an expression. Anyway, Siren vanished, so who do you pray to? You must be having your faith in someone at least. Or you are completely against all the gods and their servants like those keepers?" She sat down on the hard-stone floor. She felt immediately relaxed as she spread out her legs and leaned against the wall in a comfortable posture.

Eddie spoke up. "Yes, I was wondering about it as well. Who do you pray to now?"

Kryptal took a deep breath and sat down on the floor. Eddie followed the pursuit. All three of them were sitting facing each other. He asked Trinity, "You know the keepers kept you in the Temple of Siren, right?"

"I wasn't aware of that until now. But that doesn't answer our question."

"There were five most loyal servants of Siren. They were her advisers as well. They would guide her, before the war and warn the innocents before the inevitable dangers. They were the firearm wolves. The five wolves are the ones I pray to."

***

Hollow Fields: Midland

Sahara groaned as she got out of the glass cubicle right in the middle of the fields that appeared to be going unendingly towards infinity. There was nothing else to be seen around, no life forms, no trees, and no houses. She knew where she had come. The hollow fields. The frustrating part was to walk towards the correct field and enter the forest. And Sahara knew the guessing would take the hell out of her. And Adrian was nowhere in sight.

She started walking east of the cubicle even though everywhere around her looked the same. The walk became dry and exhausting and after a while Sahara found herself parched. Always prepared for such situations, she put her hand in her bag to get out the bottle of water that she always carried and realised there was none. "Oh shoot, I do not know how long I can go without drinking water," she told herself, trying not to panic. She had been here before; she was convinced that she would figure it out.

"Maybe we can help you with that!"

Alarmed Sahara turned around to see who that was, and all the colour drained from her face, "Zen and Zella! My two absolutely favourite people right now." Zen stood there scoffing, while Zella just threw her an icy look. Sahara backed off and started to run in the opposite direction. Zen called out from behind, "You think we didn't bring backup?"

Sahara almost ran into two burly bare-chested guys, abnormally tall with long braided hair. "Oh crap. What do you want from me?" Sahara knew she had almost lost. But if she could shoot her last shot by a proposal.

"You managed to escape last time. We will see to it that you are not even sent to prison, but you can be our direct gift to Siren this time." Sahara's eyes grew wide with horror. "But why are you doing this? What is it that you want from me? Maybe I can give it to you."

"Your life," Zella answered, watching Sahara being forcefully being dragged away.

***

Trinity quietly stared at the floor, wholc Kryptal made dinner. There were two open chambers in the ruins and in one of them, Kryptal had lit a fire in the centre, to keep it warm. Eddie was taking a nap and Trinity was figuring out if she wanted to share the visions in her dreams with Kryptal. She spoke up, "Kryptal can you tell me more about those wolves?"

Kryptal spoke in a low but firm tone, so that Eddie does not get disturbed in his sleep. "Marcus, Magnus, Valeria, Skyla and Hermit. These are the firearm wolves who were already on these lands when Siren first came. Seeing her powers, they bowed down to her and she warmly returned their respect by making them her advisers. Since then, a person with an extraordinary sense of wisdom was called blessed by the firearm wolves. They were the creators of the prophecy that one day 'the draughts will create the renegades of the most faithful and give rise to the saviour they deserved.' However, all this is a myth Trinity. None of this is real except for those monsters sacrificing innocent people."

Trinity sighed. If Kryptal didn't believe in them to be true, she had no point in sharing her dreams to him. But she felt she had to. She asked, "So, if you do not believe in all this, why do you pray to them?"

"Faith. Trinity faith even in the idea of a good thing will never corrupt you. Magic, uncanny powers, spirits and gods are very tempting concepts. But the truth and integrity are far better. It is up to you to choose which side you want to be on, and live fighting for it."

Trinity looked at him respectfully. Had she just met someone who believed in the good cause no matter what? Then it was the right person. She said slowly, "Kryptal, I have seen those wolves before. In my dreams when I first came to Sandsmid. Then I heard them every time I got into trouble as if they had been trying to warn me. And then, their painting in the cave. One thing I remember clearly that they told me in the dream was, 'Trust your heart and not the scene.'"

Kryptal dropped the wooden spoon and looked at her dumbfounded. "You are a special one. I think the only person who was able to see or hear them before was…"

"Haseena?" Trinity finished. "Because she wrote the same lines in the letter she left me."

"Hold on. You know who you are talking about?" Kryptal asked trying to take in the surprise bombs thrown at him.

"Sahara told me she was killed when I disappeared. Is that true?"

Tears appeared to be swelling up in Kryptal's eyes, but he caught himself. "She was my sister. And yes, she was killed because she was accused of conspiring against the bridge with your mother."

Trinity crawled towards him and put a comforting hand on his shoulder. "I do not think she is dead, Kryptal. She was the one who helped me in that cave before I came to Midland."

"You must be mistaken. She got burned right in front of the council. By the time I reached, there were just ashes," he said shaking slightly.

Trinity tightened her grip. Eddie was snoring peacefully completely unaware of the serious discussion that was going on. "I am not. And we will find her along with my mother. But before that, Kryptal, I need you to save my friend. She got stuck into all this because of me, and now she is suffering for absolutely no fault of hers."

Kryptal cleared his emotions and straightened up, "I do not think she has much time. She will be sacrificed on the day of the Equinox. We have to hurry."

"How many days do we have till then?"

"Five."

11.

Day One of Five Days to Equinox
Ruins: Midland

Trinity woke up with a sore back. She went to the back of the chamber to freshen up and when she returned, she found Eddie and Kryptal sitting at the entrance chatting seriously. Trinity walked up to them and stretched. "Morning, boys."

Eddie looked up and nodded at her curtly. Something did not seem right. Trinity felt the tension in the air. She sat down next to them and took a goblet and poured herself some tea that Kryptal had made for them. "What's up?"

Eddie answered, "Aella will get sacrificed if we do not reach her in time. And there is no news as to where Samaar is. He has completely vanished. We need to find him as well. And I feel that Sahara is in trouble. I haven't heard from her or Adrian at all since we arrived."

Trinity nodded meekly. It was getting exhausting to keep losing people back to back. There had to be some way of making sure of that. It hit Trinity. She had no idea what exactly the mode of communication was in Sandsmid, because as far as she knew, no one was using excessive technology. She asked them, "How do you know when the person is nearby or in another place? What is your mode of communication?"

Kryptal took out a small mirror from his waist belt. It was square in shape but almost the size of the one that Trinity had.

"We can see the face of the people who are close to us. If we do not it means they are far beyond the radar. We can say the message into the mirror and when the person is in another level, they will receive it as soon as they look into their pocket mirror."

"Jeez, that's fancy. I thought you guys had birds to send messages, you know like pigeons."

"Pigeons are idiots. And birds can be killed, or the messages can be intercepted any time. This is safer," Kryptal said passing his mirror to Trinity, who wanted to examine it.

Trinity took it in her hands and stared at the mirror. In a flash see saw Sahara's image screaming and lashing out at someone and then the visual disappeared. Trinity blinked. "So, if I see someone for a second it means they are around me?"

Eddie nodded at her his brows arched. "Why, did you see someone?"

"Yeah, I think I saw Sahara lashing out at someone. But it was just for a few seconds," Trinity replied still looking at the mirror searchingly.

Kryptal and Eddie stood up immediately. "We have to rescue her. I know she is nearby. Any clear thoughts on her whereabouts?"

Kryptal scratched his head. "Trinity did mention she was lashing out at someone. I am quite sure it was Zen's men. If we do not make it in time, they will kill her."

Trinity got up. She went inside and pulled out a leather vest from her backpack. She put it on over her tank. Put the knife in the belt and tied her boot strings tight. She was ready for the battle. She knew they would all be in probable danger if they had to face the keepers again.

When she came outside, the two men were ready. Eddie

looked fresh as a daisy and his face glowed in the twilight. He looked at Trinity and nodded approvingly. Trinity nodded back notifying her readiness to plunge blindly into the oncoming dangers.

It didn't take much time for them to reach the sacrificial ground where Kryptal anticipated Sahara would be, and he was right. There was a small crowd, yelling and chanting in a weird language and amidst them was a face furious and almost hopeless. Sahara!

Trinity, Eddie and Kryptal crouched behind one of the monoliths. Trinity could sense Eddie getting tensed nearby. The moment of critical decision was standing for both. Trinity nudged Eddie and as if on cue he nodded. His next words were cautious, careful and filled with fear. "We go now, I hope you got your knife handy, Trinity. Kryptal will manage, I think. These guys would be hard to take on, but we just need to distract them so one of us can untie Sahara. We got no time. NOW!"

Trinity closed her eyes, trying to remember all the training she had received from Adrian. Gathering her wits, she ran towards the crowd with a cry. She did manage to get everyone's attention but one of the strong men got to her before she could act. He grabbed her, lifted her above the ground and screamed something. Other keepers cried out in unison and two other guys rushed towards her with ropes. "Hell nawww. Not today, buddy," Trinity cried and sunk her teeth into his arm as hard as she could. A dreadful memory from her past flashed in her mind when her foster mother had grabbed her by her throat and pushed her into the wall, threatening to kill her. Trinity snapped into the present when that guy tossed her on the ground. She got up and took a deep breath. In no way she was going to succumb to her past hauntings. She ran towards the same guy again, and although he was ready for her, he wasn't expecting a sharp object piercing through his thigh. He looked down to see his own leg bleeding as Trinity pulled out the knife and kicked him in his guts. He fell down with a low thud. The other two guys stood there taking in the action for a few minutes before charging towards her. They got her and tied her hands behind her back.

As she was being dragged to the other side of the crowd, she noticed Eddie trying to open the knots to untie Sahara. He was so engrossed in freeing her that he was oblivious of the dangers lurking behind him. Trinity took one look and cried out to Eddie in disdain, "Watch out!" Before Eddie could react, Zen grabbed him from behind and tackled him to the ground. Sahara struggled to free herself as she realised her wrists felt lighter. "Not him, you moth," she cried in a squeaky voice. Trinity groaned. Of course, it had to be Zen. That guy must have had a miserable past, knowing how cold hearted he was. Sahara got out of her bindings and started kicking the guy who was wrestling with Eddie on the ground. It didn't work so she started jumping on the guy's face until it looked that he was going to pass out. But before Eddie could get up two other guys came from the back and grabbed Eddie and Sahara.

On the other side, Kryptal was fighting his battle with his own kind. Spear for a spear, it was getting intense. He had managed to knock down five strong guys when suddenly Zella kicked him from behind and punched his face when he turned around. Soon he was outnumbered, and three guys got hold of his spear and threw it away from him. One of them grabbed his hands and tied them behind his back. He got dragged to the spot near Trinity, who was on her knees with her hands tied.

Two other men brought Sahara and Eddie next to them and the others started cheering. The cheer died out as Zen emerged from the crowd and stood in front of them and others. Zen raised his hands to address the crowd first, "We have six valuable candidates for our dear council. Let us not burn this tiny little fairy," he said, nodding at Sahara who scowled at him and continued, "Instead we can have the privilege to watch the ceremony with all of them burned together!" The crowd cheered. Then he turned towards the captives and said in a bitter tone, "Sorry kids, you should know we do not like trespassers. Off you trot."

The men dragged these four people into the temple behind the sacrificial grounds. Trinity looked at Kryptal and whispered, "He said six people." Kryptal shrugged. Sahara looked enraged and tired. She had not resisted much when they were pushed to go down a dark pathway inside the temple. They all walked quietly. Soon they reached a huge wooden door. One of the men opened it, and shoved Trinity and her friends inside and slammed the door back shut. It was dark except for one torch burning in the corner that cast a ghastly dim glow into the chamber. It was dusty and it appeared damp with smells similar to those of a swamp.

Trinity and Sahara stood there, and they could sense movements in the far end of the chamber. Kryptal hugged Sahara warmly. "What happened to you? Where is Adrian?" Sahara shrugged. "No sign of him from the time I entered the fields. And well, Zen and his men caught me off guard in the fields. But I guess it was predictable. Burning me at a stake was not!"

Trinity held up her hand. The shapes in the distance appeared to be coming forward, yet their movements sounded filled with efforts, because sounds of the chains dragging can be heard. Then the sounds stopped. Trinity asked Eddie in a hushed tone, "That is what Zen meant when he said, 'you six'? What is he going to do with all of us?"

"Hand us over to the council and sacrifice us," came the reply from the corner. Trinity felt the sound appeared familiar. She inched closer to the source. "I think I know you."

"Of course you know me. I am Brahanne," she said, her face finally coming into focus.

***

Senge: Safe House

Michael desperately browsed through the ancient records, anything that could help to trace Samaar. He was well aware that Aella and Samaar were both captured. But Salvos probably had no intentions of sacrificing him because he wasn't in the Lighthouse with Aella. He knew that bit of information was correct as Adrian had well informed him about it and he trusted Adrian. He went to the library downstairs, frantically searching for any possible clues in the old books that mentioned where the prisoners were kept if not in Lighthouse. He had a vague hunch about Samaar's whereabouts, but he hoped that he was wrong. Safe house had a rich collection of manuscripts and knowledge about the council. With every passing second, he got nervous. Once captured, there was very little hope for absolutely anyone in Sandsmid and he was very well aware of that. The term 'justice' was perfectly buried somewhere under the dying ashes of a fair life.

As he was anxiously flipping through the pages of the

fiftieth book, he heard quick footsteps from behind him. He immediately stopped his search and crouched below a mahogany desk. Prepared to fight he looked his head barely raised to the top. The footsteps were coming closer. Holding his breath, he waited. Soon the steps stopped.

Curious he raised his head slightly. A cold hand touched his head. "AYIEEEE," he shrieked in fear and shot out of his hiding place, ready to fight. "Holy Siren, chill, boy," Dariana said, clutching her heart. Michael calmed down a bit, and then noticed Salem standing behind her. "Wait, are you really you?" he asked staring back at Dariana in shock.

"Yes, it's really me. And we need your help to reach the Midland lake. Can you come with us? My daughter and her friends are in trouble. Her best friend is in the Lighthouse," Dariana spoke everything too fast.

Michael was still having a hard time processing Dariana's presence. She had gone missing and after that no one had heard of her. Salem browsed over a few books that Michael had been reading before. He looked at a few pages in mild interest.

Dariana again pressed on, "We do not have much time. We need to save her before Salvos sacrifices her." Saying this she shuddered slightly.

Before Michael could reply, Salem spoke, "We can go ourselves, but you are our best source that can help us reach Adrian or Sahara."

Michael snapped shut a few books on the table and replied with his head down, "You will have to go without me. I am going to look for Samaar. No one seems to care about him." Noticing he was clearly offended, Dariana made an offer, "How about you help us reach Sahara or Adrian and in turn we will come help you with finding Samaar?"

Michael sighed, "I'm afraid that's not possible. I haven't heard from Adrian or Sahara for long now. And I am not even sure if they are in Midland any more."

"Please, we need your help." Salem insisted.

"Let him look for Samaar. I will come with you," someone said from behind. They had barely heard any footsteps coming in because of the conversation, but all of them turned to see who it was, and Michael nearly flipped.

"Haseena? Weren't you killed? What is with you ladies appearing out of nowhere today?"

Salem looked equally surprised. "Didn't you get my daughter caught?"

Haseena stood there crossing her arms defiantly, "No. It was Zen. I had directed her to the chambers of the temple, but you know that wretched leech. He must have imprisoned her and then informed Reh. I went back to look for Kryptal, but there was no trace of him either. We need to go to the temple as soon as possible."

Dariana went into deep thoughts. After a while she said, "Why do not you and Salem go looking for his daughter, while I go rescue my daughter and her friends. I have a bad feeling about this."

"Bad feeling?" Michael asked, curious.

"My sources said the council is not going to sacrifice just the girl. I think Trinity and the rest are going to be in it as well. We need to hurry."

12.

Temple Dungeons

Trinity ran towards Brahanne and gave her a hug. Brahanne looked weak and injured. Her knees were bare, and her dress was torn at multiple places. Her face was soiled and when she pulled out of the hug, Trinity noticed her hands were rough and bleeding. Trinity held her hand affectionately. For some strange reason, she always felt warm near Brahanne, as if she was her elder sister. After a few seconds, Sahara came up to her and asked in a low voice. "Who is the other person over there?" she said nodding at the other figure that stirred slightly.

Brahanne looked at her sympathetically and replied, "She is Angelica, she was here before me. Her condition is really bad. She has been trying to dig a hole in the ground with her hands since the day I was brought in here. I think she needs help." Kryptal rushed over to Angelica who was shaking slightly and mumbling something. Kryptal shook her, "Hey, you are safe. Now, now be with us. Trinity you got some water?" Trinity got a waterskin out of her backpack. Sahara eyed that curiously, "Where did you get that from?" Trinity shrugged. "Back from the institute? It was in the wardrobe. I grabbed it," she said handing it to Kryptal. He poured a few drops over Angelica's mouth and some on her face. She blinked in the dim light and her eyes widened when she saw Kryptal. She pushed him and sat up. "What, you want to kill me now, keeper?"

"Wait, Angelica. They are friends. They are captives as well," Sahara said sadly. Angelica looked around the room. Exhaustion was apparent on her face and behind her, there was a roughly shallow pit dug. She looked like she had gone without food and water for long and that was taking a toll on her health. After some silent moments, she stood up and cried frantically, "We need to get out of here as soon as possible. Siren is calling out. I'm afraid we do not have much time. Salvos has the scroll containing the information about the void."

"The void? That's not good," Kryptal said deep in thought.

Before anyone could talk anything else about it, Trinity asked, "What do you mean Siren is calling out?" Angelica addressed all of them this time, "Before Brahanne came, I was sitting here alone trying to figure out what was going on, when I heard the song of Siren, the war cry. They say no one has heard it in years, but these are dark times. I heard her singing and since that day I have been trying to dig a hole. Maybe we can come across a tunnel that can get us out of here."

"Wait, the song? I heard a woman singing back in the institute and minutes before I passed out in the fields, but I did not understand what she had been singing." Angelica looked at her, surprised. "Not many can hear it. But you probably didn't understand it because it was an ancient language. It was Siren herself."

Not sure whether to believe the last part or not, the group fell silent. They had to get out of there soon, because now the keepers would not give them much time. Just as Trinity was thinking over this situation, the door opened and a burly guard stepped in. "You mice better be ready, the men from Lighthouse will arrive in a few hours," he said, and left, slamming the door behind him. Angelica gasped, "If they catch us, we are as good as dead. I'm afraid they just might starve us and leave us in the grounds till the ceremony."

Trinity wondered over what Angelica just said. If that would be the case, then hopes for finding Aella would be lost. The only chance that they had. She spoke to the group with urgency in her voice, "We need to get out of here fast. Start brainstorming."

"Aye, aye leader," Eddie scoffed. Sahara rolled his eyes at him. Everyone there started walking around the cell looking for any probable signs of exit. The walls were solid. Trinity even searched for any places that might have a stud so her mirror could function. But of course the keepers were smart. They wouldn't put them in a place that was easy to escape from. She looked at what everyone else was doing. Kryptal was crouching low sniffing the dirt. Eddie had his palms plastered to the walls and was gliding them slowly to search for a weak spot. Sahara was trying to remove the chains from her ankles. "A little help over here. Does anyone have any idea of how to get rid of these things?"

"I helped Trinity to get rid of those, but I do not have my spear." Kryptal said, scratching his head.

"But you have magic." Sahara pointed out.

"It's useless here." Kryptal said.

They all thought for a while when Eddie spoke up, "What if there is a trick to get rid of them? Like a key in the wall or a lock in the ground?"

"Or a loose iron bar?" Kryptal said, noticing a small iron rod poking out of the ground in one of the dark corners of the chamber. With all the strength he could gather, Kryptal pulled it out of the ground. It was thinner than the holes in the shackles. He handed it to Sahara and smiled.

"I bet you didn't notice it did you?"

Taking it, Sahara shook her head. "I do not know what to do with it, anyone good with picking locks over here?"

Brahanne called out. "That's me. Easy peasy." Taking the rod, she inserted it into the hole and after a few seconds it opened with a soft 'click'. Soon, everyone was freed from the chains.

Angelica went back to digging the hole with her fingers and Brahanne tried to yank the door. For quite some time, all their efforts were in vain when Angelica yelled suddenly. "I found the red sand!" She showed her hands full of indeed darker looking sand in the dim light.

Everyone except Trinity rushed to her. "This means we are closer to the water channel of Lighthouse city." Trinity was just about to ask what he meant when suddenly she heard a distant thundering of footsteps. "Someone's coming."

Kryptal shouted, "If we all can join Angelica, we can dig faster. Hurry." Without any further questioning, everyone started digging with their hands with Angelica. Trinity could feel sand filled up in her nails, but she ignored that. The footsteps were getting louder slowly but steadily. They dug faster and faster. Kryptal and Eddie were sweating, and Sahara looked drained out. But no one dared to stop. The momentary escape plan appeared much more privileged than a hasty break. The sordid idea of being dragged away finally when they were close to an epiphany felt icky. All of them had become animals now, digging furiously. The footsteps were even closer than before.

The red sand was pouring out and soon enough there was a narrow tunnel that looked winding into the darkness. At this point, it was better than getting caught. Angelica commanded,

"On the count of three, jump!" "Wait," Trinity said. "If they come and discover this hole, they are bound to send their men after us. How do we cover our tracks?"

Sahara scratched her head, "Magic doesn't work in the dungeons does it?" Kryptal shook his head. "No. Plus, I do not know what we will do if the tunnel leads nowhere and the men of the bridge might catch up with us." The footsteps sounded almost from twenty feet away. There was no time to spare. It was now or never.

Eddie said, "Doesn't matter now, let us go!" and jumped into the hole. Everyone followed him one by one, until Kryptal jumped and the guards opened the door.

While they were sliding there were two branches on the inside of the tunnel, but none of them were in control of themselves and got into the left branch sliding all the way and falling right into the flowing water that dragged them right into the swampy area of the lake at last. "Ouch!" Trinity exclaimed as Sahara fell on top of her. All of them got up quickly and started walking out of that swamp. Everyone was well aware, that the longer they stayed, the quicker were the chances of getting caught. Brahanne started running ahead of them. "Hey wait, where are you going?" Angelica said but soon she did the same thing, running after her. The others followed. Brahanne looked back answering, "I have seen this place on the maps back in Midland. We are near the other side of the lake in Lighthouse city. I think," she finished excitedly. They were walking on a low lined bridge now, and sure enough they could see what she meant. The lake looked splendid, while it appeared that half of it disappeared under the hillock with an opening from where they had fallen. It all made sense now, Trinity thought. The reason Sahara had asked them to meet up at the lake in Midland was because of its continuity in Lighthouse.

Soon, they got off the bridge on the other side of the hillock and entered a chilly area. Immediately Trinity realised the temperature had dropped. Light flakes of snow fell on her hands and she saw her breath coming out in smoke. She stopped and so did the others. "This is way too cold for me. I have not prepared for this. And I do not think others have as well," she said looking at Kryptal and pointing at everyone else. Kryptal who was bare chested gave her a look that said, "Seriously?" Angelica held up a hand. "Kryptal, she is right. We can use our magic at least for a little while to keep them warm. That is one good thing about Lighthouse. Magic is allowed to everyone who practices it." Kryptal sighed. He hesitantly extended his hand to Angelica who held it and both closed their eyes and mumbled some words in another language. There was a smooth breeze around them, and they began to glow gradually. The glow manifested into a bright bubble that enveloped, Trinity and her friends. Soon, everyone started feeling warm. Kryptal and Angelica opened their eyes satisfied.

Brahanne looked at Angelica and asked, "I can understand Kryptal using magic because he is a keeper. How do you know those ancient practices? You mentioned you could even hear Siren's calling."

Angelica sighed and answered, "It is because I was born in a family practicing ancient religion. Me and my father have always been an honourable part of the 'Mystics'. They teach us the origin of Siren and where she was from. The star. The ancient language comes from that star. That is why I know the same kind of magic as the keepers, but certainly not the dark one that they have recently been practicing. And Kryptal knew that because, in a way, he knew my father. Salem."

Trinity looked around. It was now a beautiful carpet of snow and the ground they were walking on was getting elevated with smooth winding stone roads. "Angelica, where do we go now?"

Angelica looked around and lowered her voice. All of them were still walking huddled in that bright bubble. "We go to the Lighthouse library. I have someone I know there. They will let us stay and take refuge. If we need to go to the Lighthouse tower, that has the bridge council, it will not be difficult much because the ceremonial festivities have begun. Everyone would be busy getting drunk and looking good."

The rest of the walk was quiet. They crossed a tiny stone road junction and walked straight. Bright lights started to appear. Trinity, Brahanne, Sahara and Eddie looked in awe as the beautiful city loomed ahead of them with its magnificent blue, green and yellow lighting. The roads were mostly empty except a few stone mansions here and there and in the centre stood a sky piercing tower. It was a sight!

Angelica exclaimed, "Welcome to the Lighthouse city!"

***

In the cold streets of the Lighthouse city, there were three cloaked figures in a dark corner near a huge lamppost that was standing tall outside the huge stone building of the library. Those three huddled closer to each other, trying to be oblivious to the ignorant jostling guests and servants who were either leaving or going to the Lighthouse tower. Any people who they noticed on the snow-clad streets was wearing flamboyant hooded cloaks, some made of silk, some made of velvet.

The three figures lurked into the shadows of the narrow

sketchy alley behind the library and when they were sure that no one was watching, took of their hoods. Adrian stood there facing Reh and Volt. He said in a hushed tone, "Back in Toronto, if we would be meeting like this and someone caught us, they would probably think we were dealing with drugs." Looking at their confused faces, he added, "Never mind. So, what I just said, I just got here after getting out of the glass cubicle and walked to the lake on my own. I had informed Zen about Sahara, Trinity and Eddie, so they must be in the temple."

Reh held up his hand. "I do not think it worked. The keepers just told me that they escaped. We should increase the security at the Lighthouse. Anyone looking like an outsider, should be taken in for questioning. And the prisoner girl should be watched all the time. We just have four more days to go. Keep that well thought of."

Adrian nodded curtly. His expression didn't look like he was agreeing to everything that was going on. Before he could say anything else, he looked around. The ally in which they were standing was awfully quiet, but he could make out more than two people talking from somewhere behind them.

Volt's ears must have picked up on those sounds as well. He looked alert and signalled the other two to be silent. Those people appeared to be coming in their direction. "Hurry," Volt said. "We need to get back to the tower. Next time we meet by this lamppost again. Scatter."

All three of them walked fast in different directions. Adrian walked quickly, taking long steps towards the tower. He had to find a way to rescue Aella before Salvos could sacrifice her.

Trinity and the squad were walking closely in engulfed in the bright bubble. No one looked like they were willing to escape the warmth that the bubble had been providing for the past few hours. Angelica paused while entering one street and instead of walking towards the open roads that were right ahead of them, she took a sharp turn and walked towards their left. Everyone followed wordlessly. They stopped for a few minutes, listening to some people talking in the distance. Angelica signalled them, that all was clear when there was absolute silence and they walked towards the end of that alley. Reaching the alley, they reached a lamppost. Angelica and Kryptal looked relieved when Angelica pointed to a big mansion next to it. "Library, you all. We have to find Astes now."

Kryptal clicked his fingers and the bubble disappeared. Sahara let out an angry hiss. All crowded closing on to each other feeling frozen. Kryptal looked at them apologetically, opening the library door for them.

The moment Trinity stepped inside, she felt extremely warm and cosy. There was a guy standing there with half his head in a military cut and half with long hair. His one ear had a piercing, and he wore rings on his fingers. He gave them a suspicious look but nodded stating a silent welcome. Kryptal, Eddie and Angelica nodded back at him. He moved aside for them to enter. All of them went inside in a disciplined que while Angelica stayed back to chat with him. "Guys, hold on. Before you go inside, I wanted to introduce you all to my good friend here, Astes."

That man with piercing gave a little bow to introduce himself. "Hey, Astes. You know I do tattoos in my free time. Let me know if you want to get one," Brahanne said winking at him. Trinity chuckled. Even in these dangerous times, Brahanne managed to stay chirpy. Astes smiled slightly and turned his attention back to Angelica and continued his conversation with her.

Everyone except those two walked into the library and looked around in admiration. One thing that Lighthouse was proud of was flexing the knowledge house, intricately decorated with the finest of the materials every found giving it a rustic touch with an extremely warm temperature setting. Towers of bookshelves and shelves lined across the double heighted walls flaunted of the histories and their relics. Everything was made of deep dark wood and the crystal chandeliers hung low near the tables. Candles lined up onto the readers desks and the main desk had piles of parchment rolls.

Sahara knelt on that table smelling the parchments. Angelica still hadn't returned. Kryptal and Eddie were already seated around the fireplace getting warm. Brahanne was eagerly browsing through some ancient language books. Trinity was left alone in the entrance. She walked up to Sahara and sat down on the leather chair next to the table and asked, "Sahara, what's the beef with the keepers Zen and Zella?"

Sahara stopped sniffing the parchment rolls and looked at her. "Beef means?"

"I mean what issue did you have with them in the past that they were ready to burn you alive?"

"Trinity remember when we first met, and I told you that I do not trust Adrian?"

Trinity nodded.

"Well, the first time Adrian met me, in Midland, he was a charming lad with a tiny favour. I could not say no to him. He wanted to retrieve an ancient relic from the keepers."

"You mean he wanted to steal something from them," Trinity concluded.

Sahara appeared shocked as to how she was finally getting to know that Trinity could not be fooled by the play of words.

She continued, "Uh yes. And it looked like an easy job. I agreed to go with him to the Siren temple and we decided that if I helped him, I would get an access to the Lighthouse city whenever I wanted. But when indeed we managed to steal that relic from the keepers, we found out that Zen and Zella were in charge of protecting that relic with their lives. Things got out of control and they almost got killed. Adrian and I finally managed to escape with the help of a keeper who surprisingly was on our side."

"Kryptal," Trinity said thoughtfully.

"Yes him. He had been so extremely helpful. But then, Adrian and I parted ways, but he never got around to tell me that my access to the Lighthouse was granted. In fact, he never showed up after that. The time you showed up I understood that it was another of his selfish tricks. And wasn't I right about it? I helped you guys and now do you see him anywhere? He's gone, isn't he?"

Trinity sighed as she agreed. He indeed was nowhere to be found. She felt bad for Sahara. Just because she had a good heart didn't mean anyone could toy with it. She gave her a warm hug and then asked again, "Sahara, what relic did you guys go to steal anyway?"

Sahara looked up trying to remember. "It was pretty valuable now that I think about it. It was the 'amulet of Proxima'."

"Proxima as in the dwarf star?"

Sahara half nodded still unsure of the entire sentence, "Star yes. Dwarf I do not know. But yes, that is the star where Siren came from."

"And do you have that amulet with you?"

"No, Adrian has it."

Just as Trinity was about to open her mouth, Angelica came running inside with Astes closely following her carrying a lot of cloth bags. She said excitedly, "Everyone, I got all of us some disguises so we can go into the Lighthouse tower tomorrow itself when the festivities begin and Astes was kind enough to let us stay here for the night. We could all sleep on the warm carpets in the storage area and it has a furnace as well. And," she added excitedly holding the bags above her head, "some food."

Hearing the word, 'food' everyone appeared next to her in a flash. Even Kryptal and Eddie who were in the back warming themselves by the fireplace darted towards the front. Astes looked happy with himself.

Soon, everyone was sitting on the ground in a circle by the fireplace, with the food kept in centre. Marshmallows, salmon, a pile of boiled vegetables, two big plates of chicken wings, roasted potatoes, mashed potatoes, garlic bread and tomato gravy. It appeared clearly that no one in all these days had enough time or leisure to eat good food. And now, since they finally had the chance, no one was willing to miss out on anything. Everyone was stuffing themselves with all the food that was sitting there. Soon enough, the plates were clean, and the crumbs were tossed into the fire. There were no leftovers. Kryptal got up, stretched, and burped loudly.

"Ewww," Brahanne exclaimed, smiling slightly. The others yawned and stretched as well. It was time for bed. Angelica however, wanted to check on the costumes before they went to sleep. Trinity agreed to check with her, but the others wanted to do it after a nap. Angelica finally gave up and agreed to check with the others the next day.

Thick carpets were laid out in the back room and everyone

climbed into them one by one with their huge squishy blankets. Trinity felt warm. Astes slept alongside them on his bed at the far end of that room. Trinity buried her head inside her blanket, sleepy but excited about the next day. Finally, she will get to see her best friend. Soon, the lights went out and all the heads got inside their own blankets, and it was quiet and peaceful.

Trinity woke up startled, when she felt a hand stroking her head in the middle of the night. She opened her eyes to see a beautiful woman with long black hair looking at her lovingly. She put a finger to her lips and signalled her to look around suggesting not to make any noise that would wake the others up. Trinity immediately knew who that woman was. The same woman who was in her dreams before, the same one in those portrait paintings in Midland, the same woman…

Trinity could not bring herself up to recall much. Her throat closed and she tried to come up with words to address her. It was a good yet a weird feeling that made her tongue tied with a complete sense of awareness as to how confusing it was for her because she had never imagined her first encounter with that woman ever. The woman was still looking at her smiling with a hint of pride on her face. Trinity sat up and with difficulty managed to look at her in the eyes and say, "Mom?"

13.

Trinity felt wide awake. She knew that the others would be up pretty soon. There was always darkness in the Lighthouse city just like back in Senge so when the night was up, the clock in some of the people's mirror would sound an alarm, indicating morning. Trinity wasn't much surprised by this system, as it was just like setting alarms in the cell phone back at home. She wished her cell phone would work here.

Dariana and Trinity sat outside by the fireplace looking at each other in silence for a while. Nobody said a word. Dariana was looking at her daughter, taking in everything she could that she had missed out in all those years. Trinity was staring at her mother realising by every second how much she looked like her. She had so many questions but didn't know where to start. After a while, Dariana spoke, "Bluebee, how are you? How have you been all these years? I have missed you so much," she said, a tear trickling across her cheek.

Trinity filled her in about everything. Her foster parents, how violent they were. And how she and Aella had entered Sandsmid and how Aella had got captured for absolutely no fault of hers. She then she mentioned how she had not seen Adrian from when they had left Sahara's house. All the thoughts that she never thought she would share with anyone were pouring out of her. Yet she decided to keep some things to herself, like when she had heard Siren sing, how she saw the wolves and how Kryptal had told the keepers had been practicing dark magic. Trinity just wanted to take time and not rush into things because of emotions.

Dariana listened to her attentively, her eyes getting moist when learning about her enduring the pain and turmoil for most of her teenage years. "You shouldn't have been suffering. You should have been here with me." Trinity squeezed her hand. "It's okay. We are together now. And Aella will be with us as well in a few hours. I would love you to meet her." Dariana squeezed her hand tighter and just smiled back.

Eddie walked up to them and sat next to Trinity, putting a comforting arm around her. Dariana saw this and gave a sly smile to Trinity, "So Bluebee, you found someone I see." Trinity hastily shook off Eddie's hand. "No! Nothing like that. I do not want to think about anything else except Aella."

"And Samaar," said Brahanne joining them. "We've only got a few hours to prepare now. Hi Dariana, long decade no see," she said waving carelessly at her.

"And who's Bluebee? You?" Eddie said pointing at Trinity.

Dariana laughed, "Yes. That is the name that I chose for her."

"I'd like to be called Trinity though. And honestly guys how do you keep up with the hours over here? No watches, no cell phones, it's been so hard to figure out time."

"We use water clocks. It basically shows the night-time hours, but we never really have sunshine over here. Day and night both are dark. Anyway, the water fills up in the vessel slowly and when it reaches the marked lines on the vessel, we know how much time has passed. It was said to be invented by the ancient Greeks from your world," Brahanne explained and pointed at the top of one of the wooden bookshelves. There was a vessel dripping water into another vessel.

Dariana looked at it as well. "And judging by the looks of it, we just have four more hours to decide what we can do to rescue Aella and your friend Samaar," she added, looking at Brahanne.

"So, how do we do it mom?" Trinity asked. It was nice to use that word for someone that meant something to her.

Dariana remained silent for some time before answering, "We have to enter the Lighthouse when it's the busiest. Salvos and Breeman would be in the throne room for sure. The guards would be allowing anyone that has the symbol of the Lighthouse. It is like an invitation card. If you do not have it, they will pull you aside. On any other day, we would have been captured prisoners, but these days, they will not let you enter if you do not come bearing the symbol. So, it will be easier for us."

Brahanne nodded thoughtfully, "Hmm. Angelica got us the dresses. We just have to make sure that they have the Lighthouse symbol on it. And what about Adrian? He was nowhere to be seen as these guys mentioned," she finished, pointing at Trinity.

Dariana looked down hesitantly. "That is because, um he is here."

Eddie sat up straight. "What do you mean he is here in the city? He was supposed to meet us by the lake, but he never showed up. Is he a captive as well?"

Dariana answered sheepishly, "No. My friend mentioned he was in the Lighthouse tower since last two days."

Trinity looked worried. "Is he okay? Mother what's going on?"

"Kids, I have to confess something. I do not know how to make it sound simple, but Adrian has informed me occasionally on your whereabouts. And he cannot be held captive by the bridge when he is, well, a bridge member himself."

Brahanne gasped. Trinity just stared at her mother. Eddie got up really fast from his chair and said angrily, "So you were helping the bridge I see. You expect us to trust you now?" He crossed his arms.

"I do not think so," Sahara spoke from behind her. She had been standing quietly for some time listening to the conversation. "I knew Adrian was up to something, but I was never expecting him to be this horrendous."

Dariana held up her hands to calm them down. Everyone, including Trinity, ignored her. "You were on the dark side after all. Thanks for letting us know how you have been working with the bad guys," she said tearfully.

"No. I was not. And I would never. He is the one who saved you from being sacrificed."

Everyone including Trinity looked at her perplexed. "He what?"

Dariana let out a sigh. "It was three nights before the Equinox, and the ceremony was grand. With all the celebrations going on, it was hard to get you out of here, I mean, you were just a baby. And I was dead scared of Salvos. His orders were clear. You had to be sacrificed. And I didn't want you to die," Dariana held back a sob. "So when Adrian, who used to be my servant boy, came into my room that evening, I made a decision. I knew about the 'other' world. Your world now. Adrian took you away from here and out of Sandsmid. I told him to keep an eye on you and keep you out of any possible signs of dangers. But then, I heard that spies who were allies to the bridge had discovered you and you were in trouble. You might not even have been aware of that. That is when I ordered Adrian to get you here and let you out through some other exit. That would have got you in another part of your world, but at least you would have been safe."

All were still silent, waiting for her to continue. Dariana gave a quick look at all of them and said, "It was I who had opened the portal. Even the first time, when Adrian left with you, I opened the portal for him. After that, I went into hiding. Salvos was furious and I even shudder at the mere thought of what he would do if he saw me again." She shuddered and then went on, "But before I did escape, I had put in a word for Adrian to be selected as a member of the bridge council. It was the least I could have done for him. His occasional disappearance from here was overlooked because of his accuracy in the information about the borders and the world outside. Although, he too fears Salvos," she finished.

"So, Adrian is a good guy?" Sahara asked, oblivious to any other thing Dariana had just said.

Brahanne raised her eyebrows, "I think so. I mean he never really gave the bad boy vibes to me."

"That's because he never got you nearly killed," Sahara concluded.

"Okay, that's enough. Dariana, even if we do believe you, you know Lighthouse tower better than anyone of us here. You will have to take the risk to come with us, even though I know your fear for Salvos," Eddie said, trying to act a referee between Sahara and Brahanne.

"Of course I will come. I might fear Salvos, but I am even more frightened of what he would do when he sees Blue—err, Trinity. I think he knows who she is," Dariana said, her eyes wide.

"Wait, what is it that Salvos knows about me? What does that signify mother?" Trinity asked noticing everyone else's face. They were looking down, avoiding meeting her gaze.

"I want to know. Now!" Trinity demanded.

Dariana replied, "You are his daughter."

***

Salem was hurrying on the streets of the Lighthouse. All thanks to no help from Michael. He and Dariana were gratified for the help that Haseena provided them the last minute. A portal that could work across the lake from Midland. It was unlikely to cross a level through the portal he knew. If that would have been the case, everyone would have been doing it on the regular basis. But he knew Haseena had the power of the keepers and so she was able to manage some side tricks of her own. Haseena lagged walking slower than him, following his pace steadily so that they could stay away from the prying eyes of the bridge army men.

Salem and Haseena were well aware that Dariana had gone to the library to meet their daughter. And Lighthouse at the silent hour would be an extreme risk to take. Salem knew that all the bridge members would be inside the tower right now, and Reh had not been exactly friendly to him the last time they had met. So, he had to figure out where they should stay until it was safe enough for them to confront Dariana and find his daughter.

He walked faster. "Hey, can you slow down?" Haseena called from behind. "I do not think so. We can go to the ancient cathedral for now. In a few hours Dariana could meet us there."

"Salem, why can't we just go to the library instead?"

Haseena asked. It was difficult for her tiny little self to keep up with him without panting.

"I do not think we could enter the library any more. Astes would have locked it secure and standing outside of it for the whole time would simply draw a lot of attention. Plus, there would be absolutely no one in cathedral right now, so it will be open. We could get a bit warm inside," he answered, walking towards a large stone building, with an intricately carved facade showing off the history of its existence. It stood out proudly amongst other buildings even in the dark. The semi-glow from the streetlamps made it appear as if it was emerging sleepily from the shadows. Without hesitating even for a single bit, Salem walked right into the open doors closely followed by Haseena.

Once inside, he removed his long warm cloak and sat on one of the benches. "Ahh, it feels good in the warmth. The good thing is all the bridge members would be in the Lighthouse tower right now to prepare for the festivities tomorrow."

"Or they might be waiting for you and your oh, was it 'killed', partner arrive in the cathedral," said a very unpleasant voice coming from the front near the dais. Reh emerged from the shadows, sneering at Salem and Haseena. Salem, who was caught off guard for a moment, signalled Haseena to use her magic. Haseena nodded as if she understood and ran towards Reh with wooden log in her hand that she had found on the cathedral floor.

"Haseena, what? No, I was telling you to use… Never mind," Salem muttered from between his gritted teeth.

"Not so fast, my lady. We have got company." Reh smirked and shook his head to one side. Behind him came Adrian from the dark and a few men dressed in armour. Salem knew that he was screwed. He did not even bother to fight back. Haseena had stopped midway just trying to take in everything that just had happened.

Without a word, Salem and Haseena backed off. It did not take long for Adrian and Reh with their men to tie their hands and take them to the Lighthouse tower. After what seemed like walking on the spiral staircase forever, they put both of them in a dark and dingy cell. Reh slammed the door on Salem's face with an apparent satisfaction. Haseena put her hands on the bars and looked outside longingly. Salem sat in the corner with hands on his head. "I wanted to get warm for a night, not caged."

"We can do nothing now. We just have to wait for Dariana," Haseena replied sadly. She quietly stood there for some time, checking to see if anyone did come in to see them, or even diss them. She heard a soft scratching sound. She stopped and listened closely. "Salem, do you hear it? Someone is scratching the wall on the other side. Should we talk to them?" Salem shook his head. "It's better if we keep our mouths shut for now. No one can really be trusted." Haseena nodded.

Haseena went back to gazing outside silently. And then, "Salem, I think someone's coming. I can hear footsteps." She said turning back to look at him. "Wow, your ears sure are playing tricks on you today," Salem said dismissively.

But sure enough a hooded figure came up to their cell and said in a hushed tone, "Hey guys, I am really sorry about this, but there is nothing much I can do." Salem got up and curiously walked to the front trying to make out the face under that hood. The figure took the hood off. Adrian!

Adrian continued in that low voice, "I can only do what the bridge decides to do. But know that I am on your side. I will get you out as soon as possible!"

***

Trinity sat alone in silence for a while. She needed to be alone more than ever right now. The fire crackled in the hearth and the sparks flew out of the flames touching her hands as she warmed them. Her thoughts felt jumbled and revolving around just one factor. Salvos was her father and he wanted to sacrifice her.

That reason was enough to make her feel disrupted and broken. She cursed her luck. When she thought she finally had found someone whom she could call her mother, she was not at all expecting something exact opposite on the other side. She rubbed her hands spreading the warmth in them and touching them to her face. The silence itself was deafening and she wanted to scream but her voice was buried under the choked-up sobs of a grieving revelation. She closed her eyes, trying to fight back the tears.

"Do not hold them. It is not going to change the facts if you cry," said a soothing voice from next to her. Trinity opened her eyes and looked on her left side. A big grey wolf had sat next to her and was staring at the fireplace as well. It realised Trinity was looking at her and said, "Trinity, you need to face the facts and be strong. Salvos wasn't always like this. Something changed him after he changed his rituals for the prayers. He is planning something far more sinister than just sacrificing Aella."

Trinity replied surprised, "You are one of the firearm wolves, right? Sinister as in? What could be worse than sacrificing my best friend? Before it could have been me."

The wolf nodded and replied, "Yes. Call me Valeria. And

there are worse things than just a sacrifice Trinity."

"Worse things?"

"Salvos is not just going to sacrifice your friend. He has a very evil mind. Mass killings are in his plans right now," said another grey wolf sitting on her right, slightly smaller than Valeria.

Trinity stared at the smaller wolf. "And you are?"

"Hermit. Salvos is going to kill all of you, including your friends as well as Samaar and Adrian. He has a faint idea that Adrian might be a double agent. And he has the information about the void. If more than one sacrifice happens at the same time at Equinox, he may get access to the ancient place from where Siren had come," he replied.

Trinity's heart started beating faster. What she had heard was horrifying. Without further ado, she looked at Valeria and then at Hermit. "I should warn others. How will we stop him?"

Valeria answered, "Exploit your powers. You have them written in your palms. You will be able to use them in the void. The others will follow. We all shall be there when the day of the battle arrives. Now you need to wake up."

"What?" Trinity asked suddenly feeling fuzzy.

Valeria let out a low growl and Trinity's eyes flew open. Her head was in Dariana's lap and all the others were looking down at her with worry. Dariana put a hand on her head and spoke with concern, "What happened Bluebee? You just passed out while we were still talking."

14.

Trinity was still confused when she was not able to remember at what point she had passed out in the middle of the group talking. She rubbed her eyes and sat up next to Dariana. Eddie and Angelica were awake as well and sitting at the foot of her chair on either side. Astes had gone to make arrangements for snacks and refreshments before they could march to their own graves in the Lighthouse tower. Making sure about everyone listening intently to what she has to say, Trinity mentioned, "I saw Valeria and Hermit just now. They gave me some information about the bridge."

Dariana gave her an astonished look. Eddie nodded amused. Brahanne and Angelica had their mouths hanging open. Sahara and Kryptal just smiled. Dariana spoke, "You are blessed that you can see these wolves. They won't appear to anyone before their eyes. That is why you must have gone into a short slumber. They will always be on your side if you trust your heart and not the scene. What information did they give you?"

"They told me something about the void and mass killings. It is not just Aella he is sacrificing." Trinity avoided saying the name Salvos. Everyone stood there in silence trying to take in what she had just said.

Kryptal asked her, cautiously, "And why does he want to kill more than one person?"

"Hermit mentioned that he wants to get the access to

Siren's star."

Eddie said, "Then, we do not have any other option. We will be straightaway walking into a death trap. Dariana, do you have any plans?"

Dariana ordered Angelica to get some clean parchments and a quill. She roughly started sketching out the ideas, oblivious to everyone's confused expression, cleared her throat and began explaining, "So, according to Angelica, Astes manages to get us some old cloaks from the librarian's closet in the basement. So, it might, uh have been a dead man's cloak but we do not have much choice. The good part about that would be they already have the Lighthouse citizen symbol seal on them, so we can have easy access through the entrance. Now, Kryptal since you are a keeper, you will be asked to enter through the back entrance, which faces the north. All the keepers have an entry through that. Trinity, Sahara, Brahanne and I will enter through the front entrance. We will split once we go inside. Trinity, you and Brahanne will enter the west wing of the corridor, that will have the staircase to the top of tower. Meanwhile I and Sahara will look for Adrian." Sahara groaned hearing his name. "Angelica, you need to go to the shack next to the tower and look for any useful weaponry that we might need in the battle against the bridges later. And Eddie, you stay hidden near the entrance and keep an eye out for us. Any danger, come straight running inside, find any of us and we shall notify the others."

Everyone silently took in the details of the plan that Dariana had just shared and nodded in agreement. The plan did seem to make sense, and if that went right, they might be able to rescue Aella and Samaar by the end of the day.

Dariana stood up from the chair and asked anxiously, "Let

us get ready, shall we? It's nearly the time."

Everyone pulled on their cloaks in silence. It was funny seeing a multitude of colours in an old rustic library. Kryptal's cloak smelled like flowers, while Angelica's cloak had a foul odour. Everyone seemed reluctant in standing next to her. Trinity had a pink cloak while there were blue, red, orange, green and violet popping around the place, trying to find anything that they could fight with. The keepers had taken all of their weapons, including Angelica's katana, Kryptal's spear and Trinity's knife. Trinity watched as Sahara snuck a goblet inside her cloak. That was not exactly a weapon but oh well, it was Sahara after all, she thought, smiling.

Kryptal and Angelica were browsing over the old books, trying to memorise everything they could before leaving. Trinity figured out they must be remembering their ancient religion spells.

Soon, everyone was ready, and after thanking Astes with all their hearts, they walked uphill towards the Lighthouse entrance. A few people were already walking past them, whispering excitedly about the food they would get to eat in the tower and the shows they would get to watch by experts from different levels.

It was still dark outside; the sky was pitch black and soft cushiony snowflakes continued to thicken the white carpet on the ground. It was fairly cold, but Trinity was feeling warm in the cloak.

Soon they reached the entrance to the tall Lighthouse tower. As Dariana had mentioned earlier, Angelica slipped into the thin crowd and walked slowly to the shack that was next to the tower. Kryptal skipped the entrance heading for the backside. Eddie camouflaged himself with a bunch of bright yellow cloaks walking around the tower, murmuring excitedly about the stalls being set up outside. There were a few people lining up for the entrance. Trinity, Dariana, Sahara and Brahanne got in line with them. When it was Dariana's turn, she kept her head low with the hoodie shadowing her face. The guard didn't care at all while he just checked the seal on her arm, rubbing his tired eyes. They got inside without much hustle, and once in the corridor, they split. Dariana and Sahara walked downstairs on the spiral staircase towards the east, while Trinity and Brahanne started climbing up the stairs on the west side.

Trinity felt as if she had entered the medieval era, the stories about which she used to read when she was young. She would have enjoyed this time if the thought of her best friend getting burned at a stake wouldn't have kept crossing her mind again and again.

The stairs were exhausting as they kept on climbing up, defying gravity. The circular walls had a huge square opening after every few stairs. However, the space was extremely wide, and they passed a landing that had a large wooden gate, halfway up. It was chained and had a heavy metal lock. Next to it was another big window. If they stumbled backwards, one of them could fall right out of it. That was dangerous. They held on to the railing, climbing steadily, hoping no one would see them.

Halfway up, Brahanne ducked under the stairs, frightened. "Someone's coming." Trinity hid behind her, but soon realised there was no point in hiding. They would be noticed anyway. They will have to fight whoever that person was. Keeping a confident face, they kept on walking ahead. An armed guard was coming down the stairs. He stood midway facing them, and asked authoritatively, "What are you doing here?"

"We got lost. We thought there might be more food up here," Brahanne answered timidly.

The guard seemed unsure. "Hmm, I do not think that story makes sense, but you are not allowed to go upstairs. It is forbidden for the guests. Go back while I still let you," he bellowed. Brahanne stumbled back a few steps and suddenly yelled, "Run!" and ran forwards charging into him. The blow knocked him off his feet and he fell onto the railing and toppled over it, gripping it tightly and dangling mid-air. Trinity walked past him mouthing 'sorry' and climbed after Brahanne.

They soon reached at the top and saw the floor had creaky wooden planks, that would easily give way to anyone who jumped hard enough on them. This area was not fit for more than two armed guards to tread on. Brahanne slowly walked ahead and saw the end to the passage and a wide opening in the end. There was nothing else inside the tower. Trinity was closely following her. She turned around and said in a low disappointed tone, "This is wrong. There are no prisoners here."

***

Inside the Lighthouse courtroom, Salvos stood near the window looking down at the crowd bubbling excitedly. He crossed his arms and took a deep breath. His brain was completely numb, without any thoughts except for those of the sacrifice. He could not wait for Equinox. The void would be ready with the firepit to contain more than one person and he had not mentioned it to the other bridges. He turned around at his name being called, "Salvos, I think we need to get the prisoner to the void by the end of today."

Breeman was standing there, with warm eyes filled with

dread. He never agreed to Salvos's methods, but his fierceness was what kept him under his control. Even if he dared raise a voice against his, he knew where he might end up. Delivering a message to him alone was scary enough. Salvos looked at him his eyes narrowed, "Oh Breeman, dear, I am well aware of that. But Reh mentioned that we might expect company. The friends of the prisoner may come to rescue her, and you know, 'the more the merrier'."

Breeman narrowed his eyes. "But we can let our guards take care of them. But the girl needs to be present there for the sacrifice."

Salvos turned his murderous glare at him and said in a low voice with a forced smile, "I meant, more people need to be sacrificed this time, Breeman. Dear old you have grown less perceptive with age. It's okay."

Breeman stared at him in horror, "But our rituals just say one person. What would we be if we kill so many people at one time? That is against our council rules. Killing one person is bad enough, but this? Salvos, I did not sign up for this," he finished, trembling.

Salvos took a deep breath and answered, "I do not think you have a choice, old man. Either you side with the rest of us, or you join the team of those prisoners. And now, I need to be alone."

Stunned by those words, Breeman quietly nodded, turned around and left the courtroom. His mind storming with the guilt of torturing people for all these years, for the sake of power, practicing dark magic. Even though he never agreed to it, he still hadn't opposed those practices, because somewhere, he too saw some greed. His eyes burned and his blood boiled with hatred. How could he have sided with all those immoral values for most of his life? But on the other side he felt helpless. He knew Salvos was powerful. There was nothing he could do to stop him. His thoughts slowed him down and he saw a beacon of hope. Maybe he couldn't stop Salvos, but he could definitely delay him.

With quick steps, he crossed the corridor and climbed up the west wing. The steps were a lot and his exhaustion caught up with his age, but he did not stop. Steadily he climbed up the stairs, occasionally looking back that no one had been following him. He heard someone calling for help from upstairs, but he steeled himself against that cry and stopped at the heavily locked door halfway. From his cloak he pulled out a key and twisted it once inside that big lock. It opened with a swift click and he entered without any haste. There were two cells next to each other, in one of which there was a girl, scratching something furiously on the wall.

Breeman unlocked that cell and went inside hurriedly. "Hey, what are you doing?" The girl had her fingers bleeding, but it appeared as if she had stopped listening to him. He yanked her by her arm and she turned. "Holy Siren, you haven't slept. What were you scratching?" he asked, astonished, looking at her and then the wall. There were simple lines without any words and shapes. Just lines going around everywhere. He could see a huge, scratched tower in the middle of those lines.

She looked at him with tired eyes and said, "I am figuring out a way to escape. You rotten heads got me in this mess with no fault of mine. Get Trinity instead, it's her father doing this after all." She spat out the last bit and started crying, her hands on her head.

Breeman looked at her sympathetically and said, "You should not say that about your friends at least. I do not think she even knows about him. And as for us, I know we have been horrible to you. But what's done cannot be undone. I am here to rescue you. Let us get out of here fast, before anyone sees us, Aella right?"

She nodded. He quickly grabbed her by her arm and they dashed out of that cell. He could hear someone clanking on the bars in the cell next to that one but there was no time. He and Aella quickly came down the stairs and he led her straight to the underground.

The stairs ended on the rough dusty surface and it was pitch dark. Breeman whispered something and all the torches in there suddenly came to life spitting out bright flames, lighting up the room. Aella looked at him. "Is this magic?" He nodded and pointed at the far end of the room that looked like a labyrinth.

"You go out the front, you will be spotted, you go out the back, the guards will kill you. This is the only way I think will lead you safely out of this place. I do not think I can hide you much longer, you must go now."

Aella spoke thankfully, "Thank you for letting me live. I am indebted to you. I have no idea where I shall go but if at all I can look for my friend whom I so blindly cursed throughout all these days." She had regret and sadness on her face. "You know I trusted her that she would get me out of here."

Breeman replied kindly, "I am sure she would have. But you should hope she is not in trouble herself. Salvos and his men would not stop until she is dead." His eyes flashed horror. "Leave now. I am sorry I do not have enough food or water to help you through your journey but here, take my ring," he said taking off one of his rings and giving it to her, "It bears the symbol of bridge, show it to someone you trust, and they might help you out. Now go!"

Aella looked at him with gratitude for one last time, before borrowing one of the torches from the wall and stumbling towards the labyrinth, with a strong sense of confidence flooding inside her.

***

Trinity and Brahanne stared at each other when suddenly both of them remembered it at the same time. "That room with the big lock," they said together turning around and running down the steps.

They noticed that the guard whom they had pushed earlier was nowhere to be seen. Trinity rubbed her temples, wondering why they hadn't thought about it earlier. But when she tried to reason it with Brahanne, she mentioned that usually the prisoners were kept at the topmost level in the tower so there was zero chance for them to escape. The faux prison on top must have been a recent smart idea of someone.

That did make sense, Trinity thought as they reached that room. The lock had the key still inside it which made one thing clear. Someone was inside that room. Treading carefully, Trinity and Brahanne pushed the door that opened without many squeaks. There were two cells inside. One was empty. And the other one was in complete darkness. The dim lights from the torches on the walls casted enough shadows to hide the other cell completely. Borrowing one of the torches from that wall, Trinity and Brahanne crept towards the second cell and Trinity let out a tiny squeal. "I know you. You are Haseena!"

Haseena looked up and rushed towards her, her face between the bars. "Can you get me out of here please?" Trinity looked around for something she could break the lock with but then remembered the key outside. "I will be back," she said and ran out to retrieve the key. It was still sitting inside that big lock, so it was not much of a hassle for her. "Hope this guy works," she said and slid it into the lock of that cell. It clicked effortlessly letting Haseena and the other man out. Haseena ran and hugged Trinity. "Like mother, like daughter. Oh, and this is Salem. Angelica's father," she said nodding at the man next to her.

Brahanne insisted, "We need to get out of here. We still have to find Aella and Samaar. Tell me Haseena, was there someone in the cell next to you? Why is it empty?"

Haseena sighed. "If you are talking about your friend, I think it was her in that cell. But that was all. I do not think there was someone else in with her."

Trinity's feet turned to ice. "Where is she now?"

"I heard someone from the bridge council come and get her out of here just a while ago."

Trinity slumped to the ground, her head spinning. This was absolutely what she hadn't been expecting. "Who took her? And what are they going to do to her?"

Haseena put a hand on her shoulders. "I am not sure. But usually the prisoners are taken to the void for a sacrifice."

Trinity found her voice back and asked, "Then we need to get to that void, whatever it is, before anyone. I am absolutely not letting my friend die."

Salem spoke this time. "We have no time to waste right now. Let us get out of here first. I do not think she will die anytime soon. Not until the day of Equinox."

She nodded and all four of them climbed down the stairs speedily. One good thing about the festival was the absence of the guards inside. They were patrolling the grounds and the guard whom Brahanne had pushed must have alerted the others by now. They needed to hurry before they were alarmed about the intruders.

They reached the end of the stairs by the corridor. There was no sign of Dariana and Sahara anywhere. They must have given up the search when they did not find anyone, Trinity thought. Sure enough, they saw a familiar face. Dariana removed her hoodie as she glided in through the entrance again. There were visitors flooding in to look at the history of the bridges in the exhibition hall to their right. Trinity filled her in about everything that happened upstairs. Dariana's face filled with concern and worry, "I am sure Aella must be fine. And where is Samaar if he is not in here? I and Sahara came to a dead-end right after we climbed up. There have been many changes to this place after I left. We should get out of here before the guards come looking for you. I am sure they must have gotten the notice. Oh, and good to see you guys safe," she added waving carelessly at Haseena and Salem.

They started walking out of the tower with Dariana in the lead with Trinity being the last one walking behind everyone. The guards threw them a suspicious look when he saw Dariana just entering alone and leaving with a whole group withing a few minutes, but he seemed to wave it off while inspecting other visitors.

Suddenly Trinity heard the melodious sound of a woman singing, she stopped and looked around. She recognised the sound. She had heard the same tune before at the Oregon Institute. The source of sound appeared to be coming from the exhibition hall. She noticed that she was standing right at the entrance while the others had already disappeared into the crowd. She hung back and listened. The song sounded muffled, but she was sure who was singing it. She made her way to the exhibition hall.

The sound was getting louder with every step she took, and she felt that she was closer to the source. However, the people inside the hall were completely oblivious of the sound busy in reading the historical texts and admiring the relics laid out on the display tables.

There was a loud noise of a bell ringing and then Trinity saw guards running outside. She knew the guard they had pushed had alerted the security for the intruders. Trinity had to hurry. She gave a quick scan to the crowd but saw no one singing. "Okay, screw it," she thought and rushed towards the entrance but stopped when she saw three guards entering the hall from there. "Oh, no. Where do I go now?" she thought, panicking. The song became louder drawing her away from the crowd to the backside of the hall. Without giving it a second thought, she ran towards the back. There was a hole in the stone wall and Trinity went right through it.

The song stopped. The noise from the outside wasn't audible much. The room was illuminated by a red glow. She noticed that the light was being emitted by a strange red globe in the centre of that room. That globe was on a pedestal of a metal, Trinity had never seen before. There were carvings of a similar looking globe on the stone walls. She walked closer to that globe slowly, as if enchanted by it. The pedestal on which the globe sat, had carvings on it that looked similar to those back in that small room in Sahara's basement. Her fingers lightly touched those symbols, the metal glowing for a second. Her footsteps echoed as she walked around the globe.

"Ah, Bluebee is it? Finally, we meet," a very unpleasant voice snarled at her. She looked up to see a tall man, with the sharpest jawline she had ever seen in a person, standing in front of her, looking at her with pure hatred.

Trinity felt the ground slip from underneath her feet. With great effort, she kept herself together, staring right back at him with equal hatred. "So Salvos, the first father I knew, who tried to kill his own daughter. Indeed, lovely to finally meet you."

He hissed. "You are no daughter of mine. If Dariana would not have pulled that insane stunt years ago, I would have had my fallen comrades here. But it's all good. Great things are always worth the wait. You and your friends will provide a great company to our prisoners, one of them I heard is your friend?"

Trinity realised that her hatred for him was making her immune to fear. She retorted, "What prisoners? The ones we just rescued. Too bad, Salvos." She noticed that when she looked in his eyes, even in the red glow, she could see no soul in them. They just looked like sockets with painted tennis balls.

Salvo's face twisted in anger and Trinity thought he might explode. His reaction made one thing clear. Salvos did not have his men take Aella somewhere. She must have had help to get out of the prison. She waited for Salvos to burst out, but he spoke calmly, "That's fine. I have you and your friends will follow." Saying this he pointed his hands towards her, closed his eyes and yelled something. Immediately Trinity found herself in ropes that were gripping her tighter by every second.

"I will at last be able to sacrifice you. The balance needs to be maintained. A soul for a soul. Soon I willllllll..." before he could finish whatever he was saying, he was thrown high up in the air by an invisible force. As he was struggling against it, his head banged against the stone ceiling and he fell to the ground with a thud, knocked out cold.

Surprised, Trinity looked around. She saw a young girl in

her early teens with an extremely innocent face with emerald green eyes, looking down at him with her hand extended. She felt Trinity staring at her, so she turned back and smiled. Her expression was serene. She was of Trinity's height, with waist length green hair. She laughed as her hand extended towards Trinity, and her ropes became lose. Trinity wriggled herself free of those and spoke amazed, "Thank you for saving me. Do I know you?"

The girl smiled sweetly and replied, "Let us get you out of here while I still can. Your friends are looking for you. I am not sure how long he is going to be like this," she added, nodding at Salvos.

"Wait, tell me who you are," Trinity insisted before stepping out of the hole with her. The guards had given up their search in the hall and were nowhere to be seen.

"I think you have heard me singing before. I am Siren."

15.

Trinity followed Siren out of the room and into the hall. People seemed to take no notice of them, and everyone was busy either chatting with each other or looking at the artefacts reading the history. Siren was smoothly gliding through the crowd with Trinity close behind. They reached the entrance and simply walked out of there. Trinity looked around. She noticed some familiar worried looking faces amongst other people. She was about to call out to them when Siren grabbed her hand pulling her into a flash of white blinding light.

She released her hand and Trinity found herself standing with her on a plane that appeared to be made of the same metal that she had seen inside that room with the red globe. She looked around but was merely confused by white light. She felt as if she were in a bright room, just that this room appeared to be a space without corners. She noticed Siren smiling at her. Trinity asked confused, "Where are we now?"

Siren replied, "On the celestial plane. It's just a lot of white light and well, let us say like a quiet place to talk privately. A realm in the multiverse where no bad energies can disturb us for now at least. Trinity, I must warn you. The path ahead of you is going to be a bumpy ride. Trust your heart and not the scene. I will be there with you in every step, but you have to realise your own value now."

"Are you for real the Siren that I have heard about all this time? I thought you would be more like a warrior woman with a shield and you know a fierce look. But you look so innocent like a…"

"Child?" Siren finished. Her cheeks dimpled when she smiled. Trinity was just overwhelmed by the simplicity and innocence in her beauty.

"Yes basically. And I have heard you singing before. But did not understand your words. Angelica did too."

"And so did your friend in the prison."

"Aella?" Trinity's heart skipped a beat. "Where is she? I need to find her. And what about that other guy, Samaar? I didn't see him either."

Siren flinched. "I'm afraid Samaar is not in a good place. He is in the Village level. Get this news to your friends. We shall need to get him out as soon as the battle is over. And as for Aella, your best friend, let us say she is safe."

Trinity relaxed a little. "Great. So, let us all go to where Aella is. We can escape before Salvos and his men find out we are gone."

Siren shook her head disapprovingly. "Trinity, do not you get it? You were never meant to just save your best friend. You have to stop Salvos."

"You can do that. You have powers. Just let me and my friend go. Anyway," her throat closed up finishing the sentence, "I do not want to face someone who is cold enough to sacrifice his own daughter."

"Trinity, that is not Salvos who wanted to sacrifice you. There are greater dangers ahead of us. The bridge council is nothing in comparison to that. You need to know that there are things unseen to these eyes, mere myths to the mind but anomalies in the real dark world."

A sad look crossed Siren's face and she hung her head low

for a bit. "Things like?" Trinity held her breath.

Siren sighed. "Sandsmid wasn't always like this. The people in all the levels lived in harmony. There was enough bread, water and netis in the land and peace prevailed. We called our segregations of land as level because of the hierarchical standards of living. That was the same way we lived back from where I come. There were no conflicts and then followed the great war."

"Against the human invaders. Kryptal told me about it. Jeez, humans have not left out even other worlds where they try to establish their dominance," Trinity said rolling her eyes.

"Yes, and then there was nothing left. The casualties of war were unimaginable and some of ours fled into your world. And after that the bridge council was formed. And in this present day, the sacrifices that they have been doing under my name are not for me. They are just covering it up because most of the people here still believe in me."

Trinity asked, "But what does that have to do with me? Salvos tried to kill me once and well maybe today again. I and my friend need to get out of here."

Siren's eyes glowed bright while and she spoke in a deep eerie tone, "The draughts will create the renegades of the most faithful and give rise to the saviour they deserved," and she walked up to Trinity with those glowing and touched Trinity's forehead. Trinity felt a warmth breeze through her, and her head got heavy. She staggered when a mild headache hit her but caught herself in time before she could collapse.

"What was that?" she asked. Siren normalised and answered, "The ancient language. It will unravel to you with time, slowly. You are a part of this prophecy, Trinity. You have the powers of my place. Help us fight the dark forces that

Salvos is with. Or else, it won't be long before he came to into your world with them as well."

Trinity pressed her beating temples and answered, "Listen, I came this far facing these difficulties to save my best friend. And now, she is not even here. I am sorry, but do not you think this is too much to ask from me? I heard that I am special from a few people before I came here, but of what use is that if you can't even locate your best friend?"

Siren said, disappointed, "Do not you think that is a bit selfish of you to think like this? Your friends risked their everything to come here with you. Your mother, who gave up her family to save you, exposing her to Salvos and his men. You owe it to them. They took all those blows for you."

"Not me, Siren. They did it for Sandsmid. I am sorry if I have offended a goddess but get me out of this place now. I thought all this time that I was fighting with them, but now I realise I was just walking into my own death trap. I apologise. I am not the one you have been looking for."

Siren snorted. "You are not the one? Okay. How come only you can see the firearm wolves. Why are they on your side giving you advice?"

Trinity felt her eyes burn. "I DO NOT KNOW! Just get me out of here please. I am not meant for these battles," she shouted.

Siren closed her eyes in frustration. "I hope you change your mind before it's too late." She clapped her hands loudly. There was a loud flash and Trinity found herself sprawled in the snow outside the tower.

"Bluebee. Are you okay?" Dariana asked, concerned, holding Trinity by her shoulders, and pulling her up. "We were going to come inside to look for you when just a second ago I saw you coming out of the tower and when I blinked, I found you here, right next to my feet. Tell me what happened?"

*****

Kryptal was kneeling by a stone wall. His search at the back and the yards was thorough but there were no cells or trapdoors. He just hoped that Dariana or Trinity had found Aella and Samaar. He crept around the tower, keeping his head low in the cloak. There were not many keepers around yet. He did not want to appear so distinguished in the crowd just yet. The darkness did its part well and since there were not many torches in the back, he did not have much trouble coming up to the front and looking for his friends. He located Sahara and waved at her. She walked over to him with her head low and ushered him to an empty stall.

"So, what's the update?" he asked her in a hushed tone. "Everyone is here well except you. Angelica didn't find anything in the shack either. Turned out it was just a place to store the barrels. And yes, Aella's cell was found empty. We are afraid she was taken away minutes before we reached there." She sighed.

"What! That is absurd. What about the barrels? Angelica should have checked inside them," Kryptal cried out.

Sahara responded, pulling on to his arm like a kid. "No. Listen. She was in that cell and she was taken away from this place. Why would someone hide her in the barrels?"

"Who knows, she might have been hidden there all the time. And no one took her away," Kryptal argued.

Sahara gave up. "Looks like you are not going to let this go off easily. Come you need to meet someone then," she said, pulling him by his arm again towards where Dariana and the rest were.

They reached there and Kryptal saw Trinity's pale face. "What happened to you?"

"Let us say I got whammied. And that travel between the spaces made me a little sick," Trinity replied, leaning into Eddie's arms. He and Trinity moved aside to let Kryptal see, watching his face go from shock to amazed to almost in tears as he stared at Haseena run towards him with her arms wide. Angelica was also standing there with her father's hand proudly on her shoulder. Trinity smiled weakly. At least there was some good out of their search today.

Kryptal wept for a moment and embraced his sister. "I thought you were killed. When I reached there was nothing but ashes."

"I thought she got me caught as well," piped up Angelica. "Shut up, this is an entirely different case. Let them have their moment," Salem said.

Haseena answered tearfully, "Dariana had get me out through the bottom of the pier. It was a close call. The flames were so high it was impossible for them to see if I was in it or not. And Sandsmid still has some secrets unrevealed even the council. I am sorry, brother. I had to keep it a secret to protect you."

Kryptal opened his mouth to answer but closed it again. He looked content. Whatever he wanted to ask could wait. No one had noticed in all these sentimental exchanges, that Brahanne had gone to look around. She came back panting and said, "Let us get out of here. People are thinning out and I just saw some men coming for their patrol."

Eddie almost stumbled over the uneven ground with

Trinity's weight on his shoulders. They slowly strode across the narrow stone alley way leading straight to the library. Everyone was quiet on their way back each lost in their own thoughts. Trinity still feeling the anger and the shock of everything that had happened that day, and a sense of failure creeping across her mind when she realised that Aella was still missing. She still had to share everything with her mother in detail. She had just mentioned about the brief encounter with Siren, but had never gone into the details of it. Even Salvos had not yet been mentioned in their conversation.

"So you thought you could just walk around the tower without anyone knowing?" The group stopped and looked behind. Reh was standing there with ten of his men, glowering at them.

His long hair glistening in the bright snowy night. He narrowed his eyes at them taking in their apparent exhaustion.

Kryptal stepped forward, "Listen Reh, we mean no harm. We had come to look for a friend, but it was futile. We are leaving now." He raised his hand, indicating a temporary truce, but Reh was eager to kick his battle senses in.

Dariana walked next to Kryptal. Reh's eyes widened with hatred. "You! You are the reason we had to go through the wrath of Salvos. Imagine if we brought you alive to him tonight."

Dariana took a few more steps closer to him. "Fine take me, let these people go."

Reh smirked. "Sounds like you got yourself a deal."

"Mom, no!" Trinity cried, running to her mother. Reh was amused. "So, there was a bonus involved as well. How about I get you both and let everyone else go?"

Trinity stood by her mother. Before anyone could react,

Eddie ran to Reh and smacked him so hard that he fell on his face. The men immediately captured him. Kryptal closed his eyes and whispered something in concentration. A strong wind blew and some of the men tried to cover their faces, weakening their grip on Eddie, who ran back to the group. Reh slowly stood up, his nostrils flaring.

"You dare defy us!" he bellowed.

Sahara crossed his arms at him. "We just did. Go back and bring more of your minions if you want to fight us. But remember we come in peace."

Reh was infuriated. Accepting peace was out of question for him at the moment. He signalled his men to grab the group. Salem and Eddie had already anticipated this action and so they stood in front of everyone else trying to wade of the men. Kryptal was strong but Eddie was losing at the game. Soon two men got hold of him, but Angelica sprang from behind knocking both down. "What if I do not have my katana, no one can doubt my combat skills." Salem glanced at her proudly. Kryptal knocked the spears out of three men. Trinity grabbed one guy from the back who was raising Sahara in the air like a baby. She was kicking his face. Trinity kicked him and he fell to the ground, Sahara jumping on his legs. "Take this. Broken legs!" she cried leaving the man whimpering in pain. He crawled back along with a few others.

Trinity turned to see the others still battling the armed men, when her eyes fell on her mother lying on the ground. She ran to her, noticing blood spurting from her mouth. She traced the blood to the deep wound in her stomach. One of the armed men had managed to injure her with his spear. Anger surged through her veins. Her head started to hurt badly, sending vibrations throughout her body. She felt the warmth from these vibrations, seeing red everywhere. She yelled, "Hey you!"

Her voice was so loud that everyone stopped hitting each other, Reh looking at her over the mess of sprawled bodies. Trinity's eyes glowed red as she stared right through him. "You shall pay for this!" Saying this, she pointed a finger at him. Even Kryptal stopped to see this, glancing at Reh, who stood transfixed terrified.

Trinity opened her mouth and shouted, "Feel the torrid of the red flames. Burn slowly!" There were red sparks from her pointed finger and smoke rose around Reh. He had an expression of horror on his face as his clothes caught red flames. He retreated his steps. All those who were there stood in shock, silently observing this scene while Trinity still stood motionless glaring at Reh.

"Men, fall back!" Reh cried. "This is not the end. We shall meet again," he said whispering something to extinguish the flames. Soon, he and his men disappeared into the darkness. Trinity felt everything around her go black as she fell down, suddenly exhausted. Angelica and Haseena cradled Dariana, carefully caring her towards the library entrance. Trinity felt someone picking her up in their strong arms. The library was not much far and soon they reached the entrance, where Astes was waiting for them. He hurriedly helped place Dariana on a flat bed and started heating a knife to cauterize her.

Trinity slightly opened her eyes noticing that she was back in the library and still in Kryptal's arms. She felt relieved, but remembering her mother she whispered in panic, "Kryptal my mother, she's injured." Kryptal placed her next to her passed out mother and said, "She lost too much blood. We will do everything we can to save her."

Worried, she tried to get up, but her head was reeling. She

lied back. Angelica, Sahara, Haseena and Brahanne surrounded her and Dariana, looking incredulously at Trinity. Sahara asked timidly, "How did you do that, Trinity?"

"Do what?" Trinity answered feeling blank. She could only think about her mother.

"Red spell by using ancient language," Angelica finished.

***

Trinity woke up in the middle of the night by a soft noise. She woke up to find everyone else fast asleep in their blankets. She wondered what they all had been thinking about her, since she passed out after Angelica mentioned red spell. She glanced next to her to see Dariana breathing slowly, her eyes wide open staring back at her.

Still in bed, she edged closer to Dariana and whispered, "How are you feeling?"

Dariana winced. "Not good. I do not think I will be able to make it till tomorrow. The pain woke me up." Her words were strained with pain.

Trinity extended her arm to her mother. "Nothing is going to happen to you. You are not going to leave me." Her eyes watered as Dariana smiled at her and said nothing.

"I have failed everyone, mother. I am so sorry," Trinity choked trying to keep her voice low.

Worry appeared on Dariana's face. Trinity was able to see her in the semi-darkness as they were closest to the fireplace. "Why do you say this?" she asked her.

Trinity filled her in on everything in detail this time. How she met Salvos who tried to bind her and save her for the sacrifice, how Siren had asked for her help but she turned her down and how she had recited the prophecy in trance, touching Trinity's forehead and the heat she felt because of that. Dariana listened to her silently, getting lost in her own thoughts.

After Trinity finished narrating her story, Dariana said slowly, "So Siren gave you your red powers. Not technically. They were dormant inside you. She just awakened them."

Trinity slightly shook her head confused but let Dariana continue, "Trinity, you can go looking after your friend. This is our war and the last thing I would want is anything happening to you."

A wave of guilt swept through Trinity, hearing her mother's words. "I'm sorry," she whispered back.

With great effort, Dariana extended her hand towards Trinity who held it firmly. "I love you. And seeing you made me happier than I ever had been my entire life. I think this was more than I could ask for. But before I am gone, you must understand this. Salvos wasn't always like this. He was compassionate and humble, full of life. Once he went with his council member Reh to the void to pray to the gods, and when he came back, he was never the same after that. And you are my daughter. Do not ever fear the odds. Trust your heart and not the scene. I will always be with you," she finished, a tear glistening on her cheek.

Trinity squeezed her hand, letting her tears flow. "You are not going to leave me. I will do everything in my power to save you. You just said I have red powers. I will use them." She whispered getting up slowly and sitting on her mother's bed.

Dariana smiled. "No, do not. I'd rather you not waste your energy in healing me, you might need it to get out of here."

Trinity was not ready to listen to her. She closed her eyes and focused when she heard another soft thud. She opened her eyes to see an innocent girl sitting on the other side of Dariana's bed. She was avoiding eye contact with Trinity and had a smug expression on her face.

"Siren?" Trinity exclaimed surprised.

Siren kept her head low and said softly, "Not everyone is selfish like you, Trinity. I'm here to heal your mother."

16.

Day Three of Five Days till Equinox

Trinity watched as Siren took out a vial from her pocket and poured a few dark drops over Dariana's mouth. She slowly closed her mouth and closed her eyes. Siren stood up. "She just needs to rest now. She is in a strong drug induced sleep, so when she wakes up, she will be confused." Saying this she started walking towards the exit.

"Siren, wait. I am sorry for what I said earlier," Trinity said following her. It was surprising that no one had even stirred from their sleep, despite all the soft noises. The exhaustion of the small battle must have taken a toll over them.

Siren stopped, looked back, and managed a smile. "That's okay, Trinity. If I were in your place, maybe I would have reacted the same way after seeing my father talking about sacrificing me."

Grabbing a coat from one of the tables nearby, Trinity caught up with her and asked in a hushed tone, "Maybe take a walk with me?"

Siren nodded serenely. They opened the door, passing a snoring Astes by the foyer and out into the cold night. Trinity figured it must have been easy for Siren to sneak past him inside, but then again, she was Siren. She could just have appeared out of thin air. The wind howled while the soft snow carpet on the grounds kept a peaceful demeanour. Despite the chilliness in the air, Trinity felt warm walking next to Siren. The light in the lamppost was blown out as well. It was dark. The silence lingered as the entire city slept.

"My mother said you awakened the red powers inside me. What are those?" Trinity asked carefully.

"They are the powers from my red star. The ancient studies mention that not even the followers from Sandsmid could practice those. They are just passed on in the generation of one who possesses it. In your case it's your mother."

That was surprising, Trinity thought as she feared Salvos was the one with all those powers. She felt the need to know more. "In that Salvos does not possess such powers. How is he able to do all these sacrifices then? He mentioned something about his comrades and 'soul for a soul'. Can you tell me what that means?"

"Salvos does not have powers. Something is controlling him. There were dark energies back from where I came. I think he is sacrificing innocents to harness enough powers to find a way to bring those energies here. My place had a prison where such energies were locked up. That is what he must mean by those fallen comrades."

"That does not sound very comforting. What if he succeeds?" Trinity asked uneasily.

"That may not happen just yet, but yes if it does than we all fear the worse. It's the end of Sandsmid and probably your world too. The impact of the destruction would be devastating."

Trinity shuddered. "So, you think the red powers can stop them?"

Siren nodded uncertainly, "If many people with them can fight against those energies then yes. Those energies cannot be destroyed but probably we can send them back to their prison."

"So if I have those powers, then my mother shall have those as well. Why hasn't she ever used them?"

Siren laughed softly. Even her laugh was mesmerising. "Because they are still sleeping. You see, those powers are incredible, but your bodies are not designed to handle them. A mere spell could shred its user into small pieces. When I touched your forehead, I saw the pain and turmoil you had gone through in your entire life and witnessed that red energy bubbling inside of you. Not everyone can handle it. You are special. None of your ancestors had been able to experience the use of that energy."

"What makes you think I will be able to handle it? I passed out after I almost burned that guy by saying the words in a language I didn't even know. But I guess that must have been a spontaneous outburst."

"Only time will tell. You will learn to use them eventually. I know the use of those powers can be a bit overwhelming."

Trinity hugged herself. "And you are a goddess yourself. You can singlehandedly stop Salvos from summoning those energies."

Siren looked at her with big innocent eyes. "I may be a goddess to these people, because I wanted to preach peace and inspire hope for a better life. Not because I can use my powers. I sing the war cry songs to bring my people out of their despair and give them the strength. But I cannot end everything. Trinity, it's not just my battle. I can only appear on your side to help you, but I cannot change something that was predestined. My hands are tied."

"You mean to say, there is some higher power over you." Trinity mentioned curiously.

"Of course there is. Every event is prewritten. And our

destines are intertwined. We shall discuss that in detail someday," Siren said brightly.

"Oh yes, I forgot to ask you. I heard you mention it earlier. What are netis?"

"Ha-ha, you remembered that word, didn't you? You are sharp. Netis is our currency. Here." Siren produced a shining biscuit of the metal that was like that pedestal. Trinity took it in her hand and examined it. The rectangular grey metal had five wolves carved on it with a halo over their heads. Trinity recognised them. The firearm wolves.

Siren watched as Trinity stared at the biscuit in her hand curiously, saying, "Technetium. The metal made…"

"Artificially. I know, I have studied about this. Isn't it radioactive?"

"No. Not these ones. They are produced differently over here," Siren answered. Trinity handed her the biscuit, but Siren gave it back. "No. Keep it. As a souvenir. You should leave to look for your friend before it's too late. I am sure she must be near the outskirts of Lighthouse," Siren said forcing a smile.

Trinity answered feeling guilty again. "I am really sorry about all this. I shall wait till my mother gets healed and then leave." Siren nodded.

They both turned to go back when someone called from the back. "Hey lemon, who are you talking to?" Trinity kept walking. Many footsteps came behind her and someone put a hand on her shoulder. She stopped and noticed that there was no sign of Siren next to her. A face came into focus from the darkness.

Adrian. He looked at her with a sombre expression. Again, a voice from behind her said, "So you were talking to yourself, lunatic?" Trinity turned to look at the face she wanted to crush,

Reh. She saw red again. She was about to raise her hand at him when Adrian grabbed both of her hands and tied them tight. Reh laughed manically but Trinity could tell that he was still shook from the encounter he had with her before. He shouted, "Take her straight to the void." And about twenty men came from behind him and started dragging her towards the darkness.

Trinity threw Adrian a pleading look, "Adrian do not do this. Let me go. My mother needs me." She was careful not to mention about how he helped her mother in the past in front of Reh, avoiding risking her mother's life. "Please, Adrian. Let me go," Trinity shrieked, her feet kicking the ground furiously.

Adrian just stared at her helplessly with an apology in his eyes. He readjusted his facial features when Reh turned to talk to him. "Great work, Adrian, on finding her whereabouts. Now let us take her to hell – the void," he said triumphantly. Adrian nodded coldly. "Okay."

"Adrian, please," Trinity pleaded. She closed her eyes, but fear took over, making it impossible to focus on her energies. Reh slapped her. "Shut up! Adrian, send this problem away and then we can deal with all her friends and her mother."

***

Salem and Angelica were sitting by the library desk. Everyone else was still waking up. It was too early for them. Angelica had woken up when she thought she heard someone walking so she quietly crept in the darkness to the back of the bookshelves, getting herself an armchair and sitting there staring at the empty parchment rolls lying there on the desk. Soon she had been joined by her father, who noisily dragged another armchair lying nearby and now was quietly seated next to her.

Angelica spoke breaking the calming silence, "I found something when I was inside those caves before Haseena came." Salem looked over at her questioningly. She continued, "I had found the ancient texts that revealed how one can harness the energies from the void. It would require so many killings, and those spirits can be sufficient to turn entire Sandsmid upside down. I copied some of it in my journal before Haseena asked me to go to the temple. I did go there but Zen and Zella got me locked up and I wasn't able to go through much."

Salem held her hand. "Do you think that is what is in the mind of the bridge?"

Angelica shrugged. "Not the bridge but definitely Salvos. The scrolls mentioned the levels could easily be opened up and the powers can summon spirits of the great red star. Something that the wolves also informed Trinity about, the other day," she said, remembering.

Salem asked, "What is it that's bothering you? I sense uneasiness in your voice."

"What if all this is true? What if it is the end of Sandsmid? I know the bridge has men sent out to the other worlds, that stays in disguise and reports back to them. Those places won't be safe either."

"Hmmm." Salem thought scratching his face. "Was there anything crucial mentioned that would help us stop him?"

"I do not know," Angelica said, thinking hard. "It did have the mention of an amulet. That was what I had gone to the temple for. And I heard Sahara talking something about an amulet to Trinity the other day."

"Then maybe we should ask her. Is she awake?"

"She should be. It was so dark; I did not check on anyone. But most of them should be awake by now. We should also see how Dariana feels."

Salem threw her a sad look at the mention of her name. He knew she wasn't going to make it that far. Nevertheless, both stood up and walked to the back. The torches were bright and some of the people were sitting on their mattresses, rubbing the sleep out of their eyes.

Angelica's glance darted on the empty bed next to Dariana. "Where is Trinity?" she asked the confused expressions of those who were waking up. Salem knelt down and checked on Dariana. She was sleeping peacefully without any signs of pain on her face. He was surprised. He checked the wound. The clothes were just bloodstained. The wound appeared faded like it was almost a month old. He scratched his chin. There was no way it was possible this could have happened so fast. He called everyone there and all stood over her watching her sleep. It was indeed a miracle. Sahara finally realised the absence of Trinity. "Where is she?" she said looking around her.

"Maybe taking a walk around the library?" Brahanne guessed.

Eddie shook his head. "Leaving her mother like this? I do not think so. Even she had gone somewhere she would be back soon to check on her," he said pointing at Dariana. "By the way she looks far better than she did yesterday."

"Indeed. Trinity would be so relieved to see this. Where is she?" Kryptal said looking around.

Even Haseena was examining Dariana, amazed at her recovery.

"I know where she is. She is at the void."

Everyone looked up. Adrian stood in front of them with a tear-streaked face. He appeared defeated and guilty.

"Adrian?" Sahara exclaimed unhappily. "And I suppose

you were responsible for it weren't you? Astes shouldn't have let you inside in the first place."

Adrian waved his hands blankly, "Well he is sleeping."

Brahanne crossed her arms. "Why didn't you do anything to stop it?"

"Because I was the one who caught her and gave her to Reh," he replied his head hung low.

Eddie darted towards him throwing a punch in his stomach. Adrian toppled over a low-lying table and fell on his head. "I am sorry. I was helpless. I cannot let them know I am on your side."

"And so you sacrificed Trinity," Sahara said fuming. Brahanne added, "Did you kill Samaar as well?"

Adrian held up his hands pleadingly, "No, I finally found out that Samaar is in the Village. And I would never harm her. But unfortunately, she walked right where Reh and his men were, and I was bound to act like I was with him."

Sahara kicked him. "You are a bad person. You could have beaten Reh and saved Trinity instead. What was she doing out there anyway?"

"That was what I was wondering. She was even talking to someone," Adrian answered.

"Ey, you do not get to talk," Brahanne said furiously. "Whoever she was talking to, that doesn't matter. The question is, how do we get her back?"

Adrian answered, "I have a shortcut which is risky but will take you straight to the void."

"Anything to get to my daughter." No one had noticed in this commotion that Dariana was sitting on her bed, looking at Adrian.

Kryptal refused. "What? No. Dariana you are injured. We

would go and get her."

"No, I am coming, and we are not arguing over it. I feel much better. It is surprising, because the last thing I remember was taking my daughter's hand and then falling asleep."

"Yes, I was surprised at the miraculous healing as well. Not that we are so happy to have you feeling great," Salem said.

"Exactly. That means I am coming along. Adrian, what is that shortcut?"

Adrian produced a star-shaped amulet from his pocket. Angelica looked over at Salem and Sahara narrowed her eyes in anger. "That is a reminder of your ungrateful nature."

Adrian ignored her. "This amulet is the direct teleportation key to the void. All we need is the ancient recitations and we can reach there right in the central region of the void."

"Father, this was the amulet I had been telling you about. It revealed the powers of time and space travel, but in wrong hands it could prove lethal," Angelica said staring at the amulet.

Adrian replied, "True. And I have kept this hidden from the other bridge members till now."

"And that is why the keepers hate me." Sahara glared at him.

"Sahara I am sorry. There are some cons of being a double agent," Adrian said earnestly.

"But you mentioned it's risky. Why?" Brahanne asked.

"Because we will arrive there without any warnings. We do not know who would already be there waiting for us."

Dariana stood up, wobbling slightly. "I do not care, whatever it takes. Let us all get going."

Everyone started prepping and getting ready to leave. Dariana wore a thick leather vest to protect herself from the still healing wounds. Soon everybody was dressed and set to leave.

Angelica found a couple of knives and shields, giving them to some people in the group despite knowing they might prove useless against a group of people performing dark magic. But they still wanted to give their best shot.

All of them huddled around Adrian by the entrance. Astes kept a close watch over the streets, promising them to send an alert in case of anything suspicious.

Adrian held the amulet high. "We should get going before Reh and his men come looking for you all."

"What about Astes?" Brahanne asked, worried. "He is known by everyone in the Lighthouse, so he does not pose as a threat," Angelica said dismissively. Adrian nodded in agreement.

Adrian asked Sahara, "Will you like to hold the amulet with me while the others concentrate?" Surprised she joined hands with him, holding the amulet. Kryptal, Angelica, Salem,

Eddie, Dariana, Brahanne and Haseena held their hands around them and closed their eyes. Kryptal started chanting something and Angelica, Salem, Haseena and Dariana joined him. Soon the wind picked up speed inside the room, sending several books flying around. The wind began circling around them rapidly gaining more and more speed with every chant until they were completely engulfed in a tiny dust devil. Dariana yelled before dissolving in those winds, "Bluebee we are coming!"

***

Trinity felt herself being thrown to the rough ground. "Ouch," she whimpered feeling a bruise on her knee. Reh and his men had blindfolded her and forcefully teleported her with a few guards to a very humid place that smelled of sulphur.

The guard were under a strict instruction not to untie her hands. She could even feel the ropes on her ankles. They removed the blindfold and left her alone in that place. Trinity slowly adjusted to the light around and realised she was lying on the cracking ground of an open space, that roughly looked like a large crater and in the centre was a pit with red bubbling fire up to its surface. Even at a safe distance from there, Trinity figured out what that hole was filled with. Fire. She felt that she was probably near a dormant volcano, which explained the sulphuric fumes.

Trinity gagged and coughed. She slowly started dragging herself away from that fiery puddle. She noticed both her knees were bleeding and her wrists ached painfully. She winced as she continued to back off further. "So, this is the place they call void," she thought out loud.

She noticed the sky was pitch black. It appeared as if thick black clouds were completely blocking the light. And those clouds strangely appeared to be moving pretty fast. Just as she was wondering about those, she heard strong rustling winds.

Right ahead of her appeared strong whirlwinds, thick and strong enough to consume the fire from that pit and heat up the area. She watched in horror dreading the whirlwinds to catch flames, but instead of getting stronger they slowly died out.

Once, the dust cleared she saw her favourite people lying around in sand everywhere. She could hear Sahara screaming, "I think I am going to vomit. This was brutal." Kryptal stood up smiling. Dariana rushed towards her.

Trinity looked at her feeling emotional. "You came."

"Of course. What is my life worth for if I cannot save my own daughter?" she said, untying Trinity and looking at her knees.

"Oh, it's nothing." Trinity quickly put her hands on her

knees.

"Trinity, we came to get you out of here," Brahanne said eagerly. Eddie joined her. "Yes, let us get you out of here."

Hearing this Trinity stood us. "Wait, what do you mean get me out of here?"

Haseena walked next to Dariana and gave her a knowing look before answering. "Because we need to stay here and stop Salvos. I know we are not enough, but we fear this time he is going to do something that will tear Sandsmid apart."

Guilt and confusion took hold of Trinity's mind. "So, you risked everything to just get me out of here?"

"No. We risked everything to get you out of here first, so you can look for your best friend. And, to fight Salvos and his men," Eddie answered.

Trinity felt ashamed. Out of the corner of her eyes, she noticed Adrian walking towards her. "I am sorry for earlier, Trinity. I will make it up to you back in Toronto if I ever make it out alive of here. I will fight alongside your mother."

And then, something inside her stirred, sending waves of warmth. A fearless spirit was edging to help those who she knew were weak. She had always tried escaping her abusive foster parents in the past but now she had a real family. All those who were risking their own lives for what they thought was right. And she was running away from all that to go back to what? Siren was right. She was being selfish.

Tears escaped her eyes and she looked down. "Honey, what is it?" Dariana asked concerned.

"Siren was right," Trinity answered looking at the confused faces around her.

"Aella always had her faith in me. She knows I will not stop looking for her. And the wolves told me not to trust the scene but the heart. And my heart refuses to escape." Saying this Trinity sobbed with her head in her hands.

Brahanne hugged her lovingly. "Trinity, you do not have to. I know everyone told you, that you are a warrior, a saviour or someone special to save us from this wrath. But everyone has to fight their own battle. No one can lay it on someone else's head and then blame them. We understand what you must be feeling."

Trinity sobbed harder and hugged her. After a few minutes, she calmed down and straightened herself. Adrian was already holding the amulet, ready to teleport Trinity whenever she said yes. She smiled at everyone.

"Mom, and my amazing friends, in all these days, you taught me love, courage and a cause worth fighting for. I am not going anywhere."

"But Trinity, we need to get you somewhere safe at least. Salvos will sacrifice you otherwise. Or worse you may get injured badly in this war. None of us guarantee safety once the war started."

"Something tells me the red powers were given to me for a reason. If I do not use them now, I do not have any right to own them," Trinity replied looking boldly at everyone. No one said anything, except her mother, who mumbled, "I'm proud of you."

"Adrian, how come I never doubted your betrayal towards us?"

Everyone stood there. Fear struck as Salvos, Reh, Volt and Breeman walked towards them slowly with almost a hundred men in armour following them.

17.

Trinity bravely stepped in front of her friends and face those council members, "At least he was in his right mind. Give up, Salvos. It's not worth a bloodshed."

Salvos scowled at her. "Dare you speak to me like this! Bloodshed is what this is all about!"

Trinity stood her ground. She could feel the others behind her shift uneasily. She bellowed, "Yes I dare. And remember, balance. Your dark deeds need to end. Because of your cruel acts, I never got the childhood I deserved. Never got to be with the person who loved me the most." She glanced at her mother.

Reh said irritably, "Skip the small talk. Men, seize them!"

The clouds over the crater shifted rapidly and the pit spurted bubbling fire around it. It hissed as it touched the ground. The strong sulphuric stench made the tension nastier. Both the sides had people staring fearfully at each anticipating the other's moves scared of an imminent attack. Salvos glanced behind him announcing, "Let us not wait for the day of Equinox then. The gods will be happy for my early offering."

The men behind him roared loudly in unison. Their cries were deafening, that shook Trinity. She knew she had to go by her instincts, there was no time to come up with any plans. She braced herself as those men came running towards her friends, with their spears raised in the air. Before she could react, two strong hands grabbed her and dragged her towards the pit. She looked behind, trying to get off them. Dariana, Sahara and the rest of her friends, including Adrian were struggling against those men. But she knew sadly who had an upper hand in this battle. They were easily outnumbered and helpless against the skilfully armed soldiers.

Salvos walked over to still captured Trinity, raising his hand to silence the noise. "Let us start with Bluebee. Long live Siren." Reh and Volt repeated that loudly after him. Breeman stood there frozen for a minute before raising his hand and addressing Salvos, "I am not sure I can stand alongside your crimes any more. As a respected council member, I ask you to release all these innocents present over here. We can avoid unnecessary chaos."

Reh snorted. Instead of Salvos, he replied, "You old pig! You thought you would give us a command and we will all follow it? It took years for us to come to this point! Either close your eyes if you can't watch it or you are free to join them."

Everyone stood there shocked at his words. Even the soldiers did not move. With Reh's harsh words still echoing in the sultry air, Breeman quietly walked over to where Adrian stood with his hands bound and grabbed a spear from the nearby soldier. Volt screamed, "Grab him!"

Three men grabbed Breeman, snatching the spear out of his hands and tossing it away. They dragged him near Trinity. Salvos bellowed, "Behold, a lesson for those who go against us." Then looking at the sky, he raised his arms wide, screaming, "Siren, accept my offerings," and glanced at the soldiers holding Breeman and Trinity, commanding, "Toss them."

Just as they were about to lower Trinity into the pit, she yelled, "Wait!" the soldier stopped. Salvos looked at her with narrow eyes. Trinity looked over him to see Dariana, who had a murderous glare on her face, Adrian had his hands curled into fists, and Kryptal already closing his eyes. She turned her attention to all of them yelling, "This man is a liar! He is not offering his sacrifice to Siren. Salvos you are a hideous pretender."

Salvos shouted, "Now!"

"No!" screamed Dariana from behind. Eddie, Kryptal and Adrian tried to shake off their captors vehemently, but in vain. They stood there helpless watching painfully as the soldiers raised Trinity above the pit. She threw one last look at her friends and then closed her eyes, taking in the warm vapours from the hole. "Siren, take care of my friends." She felt the hands letting her go. But instead of feeling extremely hot flames on her body, she experienced a sense of immensely comforting warmth. Something inside her stirred again, the waves reverberating throughout her body. Her vision faded and everything started to make sense. The flames were just fuelling her red powers. She shot out of the pit, hovering a few feet above the bubbling fire. She could see everything ten times clearer than before with a red glow to the surrounding.

Her eyes darted from Salvos to Reh. Breeman was still held close to the pit. But hadn't been thrown inside yet. She noticed horror on Reh's face while Salvos stood unnerved. She thundered, "You thought I came all the way to Sandsmid just to die that easily? I do not think so."

There was a sharp whirlwind and five figures dropped out of it. Zen, Zella, and a few of their evil associate keepers. Trinity watched as they rushed next to Salvos, Zen closing his eyes in frustration when he saw her. Salvos retorted, "No I never expected it to be easy. That is why I brought some friends who can help me fight your red powers."

Zen was just about to make a move towards her when there was another whirlwind, followed by another and then another. Soon the place was swarming with people who appeared to be powerful personalities, one of them siding with the captured people before shouting, "We are all here to fight you Salvos. Your time is up!" "Yes," a hundred others repeated. Soon, there were enough people to fight Salvos and his army.

This shook Salvos for a second. Volt stammered, "H-how?"

One man who was studded head to toe with jewels replied, "The war cry. We heard the song of Siren and all of those who are present here understood what it meant. That is what got us here."

Even Breeman was surprised. He called out to that man, "How did you know where to come?"

A lady came next to that man and replied looking icily at Zen, "This is where everything started. The beginning of Sandsmid, now will be the end of the bridge. The war cry was sung first in this place. This was the place where Siren landed, and it was the birth of Sandsmid."

Still floating, Trinity roared, "People of Sandsmid. The bridge has been fooling you till now. They do not pray to Siren. They pray in her name to hide their sacrifices that they offer to the fallen Flarel Deterium. The dark entity that consumes the souls to unveil the space travel to his planet. Remember, Siren wouldn't have wanted this."

Trinity was surprised as these words escaped her mouth. She realised the red energies were enabling her to access the ancient knowledge. She closed her eyes again and felt herself touching the ground. Immediately her feet touched the surface. She opened her eyes and swiftly grabbed a spear from the nearby soldier, raised it in the air and screamed, "Charge!"

People from both the sides ran towards each other screaming loudly. Trinity ran to her mother and kicked the man who was holding her into his guts. He shrieked in pain and let go of her. Dariana hugged her tight and went to rescue Haseena and Sahara who were helplessly flailing their arms against the men who were holding her. Another woman joined Dariana and together they managed to pull those two ladies out of the soldier's clutches.

Trinity looked around her, hopeful now that they were equally numbered against the council and their men. She knew what she had to do. She needed to take care of Zen and Zella, who were shouting spells that made dark smoke pipes pierce a few people's bodies, leaving them bleeding profusely.

She caught Zen's hand when he raised it at the jewelled man who had spoken earlier to pierce his heart and yanked him. Zen howled in frustration as Trinity threw a fist in his face and screamed, "Pleasing the pain of others, taste your own with your skin." And to her surprise, he backed off his skin burning in red vapours. "Yaaarhhh." Zella ran screaming towards her. Trinity swiftly ducked throwing her aside with a strong kick and smiled. Adrian's combat training was finally being put to a good use. She watched as Zen and Zella seethed in agony, rolling on the ground.

Someone from the back grabbed her by her hair. "Ouch!" she said, turning back to see two strong soldiers pointing their spears at her. Trinity closed her eyes, letting the red energies take over. The next thing she knew was she was sending red sparks from her hands into their eyes. They threw their spears, screaming in pain. She looked over again to see how her friends were dealing with the bad guys. Kryptal and Volt were having a furious energy battle where they were pointing their hands at each other yelling spells and throwing light beams at each other. One of those beams went through Volt's shoulders, who winced as he lowered his hands. Two other people from behind kicked him in the back and he fell to the ground. Haseena was equally occupied with casting spells over three soldiers, as physically she was no match for them. She noticed Eddie was lying on the ground unconscious with blood on his legs. Trinity frowned, worried. People were getting injured and the army was proving to be more resistant than she had hoped. Her skin crawled as she saw five more people fall to the ground bleeding and almost lifeless. Sahara's scream led her to see four guards kicking her tiny little form on the ground. She lost it. "Hey, you losers!" she called out to them. One of them turned and she smoothly grabbed his spear and pierced his shoulders, kicking the other guy in his stomach. They fell back but Sahara was already unconscious.

Trinity watched in worry as more and more bodies flopped on the ground, some gravely injured, while some already on the verge of death. This was not good. Innocent people were dying. She made her way to Salvos, escaping the blow of two of his men, getting bruises on her face in the process. Salvos was battling a little boy whom he picked up and roared a few words at, black smoke taking hold of that boy and entering his ears. His screams shook her to her bone as she pointed her hand at him and yelled, "Free the fall!" in ancient language. Immediately the black smoke dissolved, and the boy's fall was cushioned by a small red cloud.

"Salvos!" Trinity called out to him. "This is enough. Innocent people are dying. Just give up."

Salvos snorted. "I am not Salvos! Call me Flarel. Lieutenant

Flarel. And now no one would be able to stop me." Saying this he rushed towards the pit and closed his eyes shouting, "This is Flarel. I call upon all the dark energies of Xanas, come to me from the depths of the Flux." As soon as he said this, all the dark clouds that Trinity had been observing rushed towards the pit. Strong winds blew as those dark clouds funnelled into the pit.

Fear gripped her, but she tried to shake it off from her head. She closed her eyes praying to the red energies to help her out. When she opened her eyes, she saw an image of an innocent girl with green hair in front of her. Hope filled Trinity and she closed her eyes again focusing with all her strength. Her legs felt light as she levitated a few metres above the ground again. She opened her eyes again to notice Siren floating next to her smiling encouragingly. "Give me your hand," she said softly.

Trinity did as she was told. She felt strong currents surge through her when her hand touched Siren's. She took a deep breath and shouted, "Flarel! On behalf of the government on Prima you are condemned to the core for all the crimes you have committed. We will not let you destroy Sandsmid. This is the land for those who want to live a peaceful life. Thereby, in the presence of our holy firearm warriors, we send you back to the prison you came from. Be gone!" Trinity her voice was powered by a stronger voice, Siren's. She opened her eyes to watch Salvos frozen in his place.

There was loud thunder and lightning shook the grounds. Trinity saw five huge silhouettes of wolves in the sky when the lightning struck. The dark energies funnelling in the pit seemed to pick up speed, and to Salvos's horror, he started getting sucked into that pit with those clouds. Reh desperately held on to him to prevent him from ending up with the energies, but the pull was too powerful. To Trinity's surprise a dark entity escaped Salvos and got sucked into the funnel.

He collapsed to the ground as the energies completely merged with the lava, some of it spilling on the ground hissing furiously and then, all was calm.

The thunder struck again, and Trinity saw a large transparent form of Valeria looking at her nodding approvingly before disappearing. Trinity slowly touched the ground and turned to everyone. Even Volt and Reh were cowering next to unconscious Salvos. Breeman stood up, balancing his bleeding arm with his other hand and addressed the now confused horde. "The evil has fallen and the good wins!" the crowd cheered. Even some of the soldiers joined them. He raised a hand to silence them. The cheer died down. He shouted again, "Bluebee is blessed by Siren herself. I, Breeman declare the end of the bridge council from this very moment. We are at your command Bluebee!" he said looking at Trinity. Loud cheers erupted from the crowd again. Trinity could see Salem holding bruised Angelica's hand cheering along with the others. Dariana stood in the front limping, happily screaming for her daughter.

Trinity smiled and stepped in front of the crowd. "Actually, I go by Trinity," she said correcting Breeman. He nodded warmly. She continued, "And I name the rightful governor for these peaceful lands. Dariana and Haseena are my valued leaders and guides. I am handing over these lands to them. I have a lot to learn yet. But I will always be willing to lay down my life to protect Sandsmid," she said bowing down to the crowd. She was shortly joined by Haseena and Dariana.

Some people acknowledged while the others murmured amongst each other, discussing whether they should accept them as their leaders or not. Dariana announced, "I am honoured, Trinity, to have you as my daughter." She glanced proudly at Trinity and then continued, "Now, the wrongdoers shall be imprisoned. I humbly request Salem and Kryptal to guide us through our new journey. And I promise, from now on, not a single soul will be sacrificed."

Loud claps erupted from the crowd. Everyone agreed to letting the wife of a former bridge member rule the lands. All were aware about the stories of her saving her daughter. People seemed to agree with the decision. Trinity glanced as Reh and Volt slowly dragged Salvos's unconscious body behind the pit to escape, so she yelled, "They are escaping!" The soldiers who were obeying the orders of Salvos ran towards Reh and captured all three of them before they could teleport. The rest of the army marched forward and stood behind Dariana and team.

Trinity happily looked at her mother, who was ordering the soldiers to help the injured. Trinity walked around the bodies, trying to locate her friends. She noticed some people were kneeling over their dead loved ones, some were trying to help the injured, while some were teleporting back to their homes. The boy whom she had saved from Salvos earlier appeared to be holding an older lady's hand as they slowly got engulfed in the whirlwinds. She rushed over to where Sahara was lying. Some soldiers picked her up gently and carried her to place her with the injured others. Brahanne and Eddie were conscious now, sitting up and happily looking around realising they had won.

Trinity was about to walk towards them when someone tapped on her shoulders. She turned to see Siren innocently smiling at her. Trinity crossed her arms and pretended to sulk, "So you tricked me into getting caught, huh?" Siren shook her head. "The walk was your idea, remember?"

"So why wasn't anyone else able to see you?"

"Because they can't. They can hear me though. So, I just wanted to say that you are not selfish after all."

Trinity looked at her respectfully, "I wouldn't have done it without your help. Thank you."

Siren waved her hand dismissively. "Do not thank me. You overcame your fear and prioritised what needed to be done. You are indeed a rightful leader. But as you said, you have a lot to learn."

Trinity nodded with a wide smile. "Indeed. Let us start with Prima. Why did we say Prima when your star is Proxima?"

"Because that is our sun. My planet is Prima that revolves around that star which acts as our sun."

"But I always thought you were born out of the star. Even the amulet?" Trinity asked confused.

"The star is an ancient depiction of power. That is how our planet can have life, because of Proxima. Just like Earth is habitable because of your sun. And also the correct distance. To be honest, let people think that I was born out of the star, makes me a little more interesting. Do not you think?" She winked at Trinity.

"Trinity, can you help your friends reach to the Lighthouse? I am going to stay back to help those who are injured." Dariana called out from the back.

"Coming," Trinity replied distracted watching Siren walking slowly around the fallen looking sadly at their lifeless forms. There were not many, but she sadly touched their heads kneeling down.

Trinity turned her back to Siren and started heading towards her friends, when she heard a soft singing sound. This time she could understand the words,

"Do not you cry, I am by your side,
Sleep, sleep my children you fought well,
The waves of light are high on tide,
They will take you where I dwell,
Stars can rise and fall,
With their red light, shining bright,
Happy fields reside far beyond that wall,
Do not grieve, I will be your ride."

Trinity turned to see Siren walking around those fallen singing sadly. She noticed that Siren's feet were bleeding as she smiled at her with sadness turning into red smoke along with the other bodies. She recalled about what Kryptal had once told her. How Siren had walked the lands barefoot, singing for her people. She appeared to be doing the same, praying for those who had laid down their lives to save Sandsmid in the battle. Soon, there was nothing on the ground where she stood.

Trinity ran to her friends who were getting ready to teleport back to the library. Dariana and Haseena were still helping others. Adrian walked over to Trinity and whispered, "I know you had been talking to Siren this whole time." Trinity looked at him and smiled. "Wasn't that obvious?"

The whirlwinds began to rise around them. The winds picked up speed when Trinity heard an echoing voice realising it was Siren's, "See you soon, saviour."

18.

Trinity rested on the red velvet armchair with Sahara and Brahanne. Eddie was curled up on the couch next to theirs, dozing peacefully. It had only been a few hours after they had reached the Lighthouse tower. Dariana and Salem, along with the others gradually helped everyone through into the lower halls, that now had beds on which they laid the injured. Kryptal agreed to stay there and take care of them. Haseena had volunteered to brew the medicines to help with their healing.

Astes had come to the tower with all their belongings. He was placing them next to Eddie's couch. Adrian, Dariana, Salem and Breeman were having a meeting the council room right above theirs. Angelica was in the weaponry shack near the tower, looking for a suitable sword for herself. Trinity felt exhausted but relieved. Her mind was elated by the recent events despite the sadness of the aftermath in the void.

Zen and Zella along with their helpers were locked up safely on the top with heavy security and patrolling guards. Salvos, Reh and Volt were in the dungeons, chained. The new leaders were still wondering what to do with them.

"Now what?" Sahara asked lying across Trinity. Trinity stretched out her arms and yawned. "Now, I will leave soon for finding Aella."

Brahanne sat up. "You mean you are not going to stay here with your mother and watch her rule for a few days? I mean you are not staying back to enjoy the royalty?"

Trinity sighed. "Every second wasted is a second I lose in looking for my best friend. She had her faith in me, and I should not let her down. I do not even know what condition she will be in right now."

"Then you should start by looking around for clues in the tower. Maybe you might find something that will give you a lead to her," Sahara suggested.

"And I will come with you," said Brahanne, standing up and glancing out of the opening of their hall. The sky was blue now and the snow glistened in the lights from the streetlamps. Everything appeared peaceful.

Trinity looked at her in surprise. "That's, um. Brahanne you do not have to. I do not even know how far I will have to go to look for her."

Brahanne replied casually, "Listen, I have always spent my life running and hiding from the law. That is why I was always alone. It has been rightfully said that the longer you stay alone, the longer you remain alive." There was a gruff noise. Eddie had begun snoring loudly.

Brahanne threw up her hands. "Anyway, what I mean to say is, it would be nice to stay with someone for a change."

Trinity's heart melted. She always liked Brahanne but now she knew for sure why. Brahanne was definitely like her sister. "I would love to have you as well." She smiled at her.

"Then I want to come to," Sahara piped up. Trinity and Brahanne looked at her. "No, Sahara. What about your deal with Adrian for Oregon Institute?" Trinity asked.

Sahara laughed, "Adrian has to give it to me. If not, I am going to your mother." She looked at Trinity.

Trinity snickered. "That would be fun to watch. But yes, you need to get that first. I do not want you to risk your life."

Sahara replied, "I agree. It would be fun indeed. No, Trinity. I figured just lying Brahanne. I stayed hidden for way to long. Now is my time to explore and what more do you need when you get to do it with your two awesome friends," she said holding out her arms. Trinity and Brahanne rushed in for a group hug.

Trinity smiled thinking how she had been fortunate enough to make such selfless friends. She told them, "I need to ask the guards if anyone saw Aella escaping. Someone might be able to give me some information."

"I might be able to." The three girls looked over at the entrance of the hall. Breeman was standing there with Adrian.

"Trinity," he said. "I have a confession to make about your best friend."

***

Trinity panted as she and the others got down through the stairs below the main floor. After Breeman explaining to her how he had helped Aella escape she had been furious with him for a while. "You should have mentioned that earlier. She could be in some trouble right now," she had wailed at him. Breeman, apologetic, had led her to the staircase that went straight below the ground.

By now, Trinity and her friends had realised that Lighthouse tower was an addition to the entire mansion that they called the part of the tower itself. All the council meeting rooms were in the towers, while the halls and the kitchens were downstairs. When Trinity, Dariana and team had entered before it was obvious for them to miss that staircase because of its location that deferred from the one that had taken them to the faux prison on top. Furious with herself for missing out on that detail, she followed Breeman, her feet making clip clop noises on the stairs.

Dariana, Adrian, Brahanne and Sahara were right after Trinity. Trinity's feet touched the solid dusty ground, and she strained her eyes to make out through the space in darkness. Breeman fetched a candle. "Wait, do not light it up," Trinity said closing her eyes and focusing on fire whispering, "Red blaze," softly in the ancient language and a bright red flame shot up from that candle.

Brahanne gripped her shoulder from her back saying proudly, "Been working on your skills, haven't you?" Trinity laughed, "Not much. I still do not understand when my tongue switches to ancient language. I need to understand it first."

The flame was bright enough to light up the entire underground chamber. Breeman pointed at the far end and Trinity could see the labyrinth. He said, "This leads to the outskirts, but after that no one really knows where it ends."

Trinity slowly walked closer to it, taking in the smell of fresh moss, wet mud and cold humid air. "Any speculations?" she asked him.

Breeman spoke, "Not that I know off. This labyrinth was hidden by a stone wall. But just a few months ago, I was down here to inspect this place by Volt's suggestion to turn it into a potential storage area when I noticed a crack in the wall and accidently discovered this place."

Dariana questioned, "And then?"

"And then, I reported of the moisture and humidity, so no one ever thought of coming down here. I used to come down here to break that wall bit by bit gradually, but alone. Soon when I found it, I figured the direction in which it leads to goes straight to the outskirts of Lighthouse, but I am not sure if you can cross the levels after that."

Trinity asked hopefully, "Then, we are not so far from finding Aella."

Dariana answered sincerely, "I am not sure about that."

Sahara said, "I agree with Trinity. When do you want to leave?"

"Maybe after a few hours," Trinity replied. "Breeman, thank you for saving my friend. Although it hurts to think about how we just missed each other by minutes."

Breeman bowed his head. "I understand. Now you must prepare for your journey."

Trinity turned around and started climbing up the stairs. Others followed. Breeman still had the candle in his hand and one of his sleeves was on fire because of the flame but he was climbing up the stairs completely unaware of it. "Breeman, your sleeve!" Brahanne pointed out. He realised this and vehemently blew on the burning sleeve. Sahara on reaching the exhibition hall, ran to get water while Brahanne put a heavy cloth around his hand to stop the fire from spreading.

Dariana walked up to Trinity while all of this was happening and whispered softly, "There is someone I want you to meet. Come with me."

Wondering what her mother wanted to show her, she silently followed her. Dariana walked up to where the council room was located and then instead of stopping there, she headed to the east side of it. Surprised, Trinity followed her quietly. Her steps echoed in the tall narrow stone walled corridors as she and her mother approached nearly the end of it. There was a huge wooden door lined with yellow gold. Dariana pushed it open and walked inside, her daughter right after her.

The room was already bright with candles and torches everywhere. Trinity noticed a golden crib right at the front of the room. There was a large bed in the distance right next to one of the windows. Metal statues decorated the room with flowers growing in the vase that sat in the centre of the room. There was a painting of her mother holding a baby right in the centre of the farthest stone wall. Trinity stammered looking at her mother, "This… this…"

"Was our room." Dariana replied patting her lovingly. Happy, Trinity stepped in walking towards the bed, where she noticed someone frail looking lying silently.

She looked at her mother questioningly, "Mother who is that?"

Dariana sighed. "That is your father. Salvos."

Trinity's throat went dry. She looked at Dariana furiously. "Why is he here? Shouldn't he be in the prison. Tell me a good reason why I should not throw him out of that window," she said pointing at the window next to which he was lying.

Dariana took Trinity's hand and squeezed it. "I am not going to give you any reasons. Listen to what he has to say first. Then do whatever you want."

This relaxed her. She and Dariana walked up to the bed and sat on its edge next to him. He slowly opened his eyes, "Is it you, Bluebee?"

Trinity rolled her eyes. Her mouther mouthed, 'Be nice,' and she replied, "Well you nearly killed me twice, so you should know it's me. And I go by Trinity now."

Salvos extended his hand for her to hold it. Hesitantly she took his hand and felt his fragile brittle skin. Before anyone could say anything, Salvos started weeping. It was different to see him from his menacingly frightening profile to a weak man bawling his eyes out. Not knowing what to do, Trinity just stared at him. After a while he stopped crying and looked at Dariana and Trinity and said, "I did not try to kill you. That wasn't me. I was hosting a parasite. A fallen spirit from Prima called Flarel. When I went with Reh the first time to the void, he already had made a sacrifice before and unaware of his intentions, I agreed to call upon the energies from the depth of a dark prison called Flux. I had no idea what I was getting myself into. I was usually a strong-minded person, but that year had been bad for Sandsmid. Famines and droughts drove my people crazy. In a desperate attempt to save my people, I did whatever idea Reh proposed without truly analysing the cons for using dark magic. He told me it would immediately affect the draughts."

Trinity took back her hand and crossed her arms. "Then why didn't Reh host the parasite himself?"

Salvos smiled weakly. "Evil needs a face. And a puppet who can pull the strings. I was the face and Reh was the puppet. He knew about the Flux and he was determined to exploit it. He made me the face of evil because I knew people feared me for my strong decisions anyway, so it was easy for them to believe that I am the bad guy."

Dariana asked, "So that's why you, I mean Flarel, killed so many people, to replace the spirits in the Flux to maintain the balance?"

Salvos nodded. "Those black clouds over the void? They are the spirits escaped in exchange for the spirits offered. As soon as all of them would be out, they would need plenty of hosts to enter our world, and so they can bring annihilation upon Sandsmid."

Trinity asked, "How did Reh know about all this?"

"I do not know. Because after I was possessed all I felt was fighting against an alien force inside my head, screaming for help but he threatened to harm my physical form every time I tried to win over him in my head. So I was never able to ask anything that I wanted to know. It's a good thing now that he's locked up."

He lowered his head and wept again. "I am so sorry, Trinity. And Dariana, I love you both. I would never have done anything to hurt you ever. I do not know what I would have done without you." The tears were pooling out wetting the sheets. Trinity put a hand on his shoulders and looked in his eyes. "It's okay. You did not know what you were doing. Do not waste your energy right now. You need to heal. Flarel has left you weak."

But he kept on crying, "I do not know how I will make it up to all the years that you suffered because of my actions."

A deep sense of calm settled in Trinity as she looked at him comfortingly, saying, "You have the rest of your life to make it up to us." He smiled from between the tears at her. She smiled back warmly.

"You should get ready now. You have to leave in a few hours," Dariana said putting a hand over hers. Salvos's smile faded a little, "You are leaving already?"

Trinity sighed. "I have to. There is something important I need to do," she replied, thinking about the labyrinth when a thought crossed her mind. "Mother, you expressed your uncertainty at the possibility of finding Aella by the outskirts, why?"

Salvos looked from Trinity to Dariana confused. Instead of talking to him, Dariana answered Trinity, "Because I have studied the ancient religion. There was a mention of a labyrinth that led to the oasis of silver to the centre of the earth."

"You mean our Earth," Trinity spoke. Dariana nodded. "The point where all the boundaries of our worlds merge into one."

"What is there in that oasis? Is it just silver?"

Dariana shook her head smiling. "Answers. And access to interdimensional worlds. You need to learn about the energies you got from the red star. Learn your legacy. It has everything. The bountiful of silver houses the secrets of the universe. You will soon realise how primitive the people of Sandsmid, and Earth are. But…"

"But what?" Trinity asked engrossed in whatever her mother was saying,

"But no living being has made it till there. It houses the most dangerous regions and creatures of space and time," Salvos replied.

Both Trinity and Dariana looked at him. "What? I also studied ancient history. Maybe not the language but my studies did mention a brief description about the oasis. Be careful, daughter, may Siren be with you."

Trinity smiled. She low-key knew Siren would always be with her no matter what. She felt a soul connection with her.

"But beware. This labyrinth will show you a way into a giant maze that might lead you in and out of this world. There are many portals unexplored, some leading back to your world, some leading elsewhere. And who knows, maybe you might find Rheora herself," Dariana finished.

"Another goddess?" Trinity asked sceptically.

"Not exactly. She is the eternal oracle. Her tears created the oasis of silver."

Trinity got up. "Right that makes sense," she said jokingly.

Dariana caught her arm. "Be careful please?"

"I promise I will. What will you guys do now that the bridge is dissolved?"

Salvos replied, "I will study as much as I can to stop people like Reh and heal."

Trinity nodded now looking at Dariana. "And you?"

She got up smiling, "The democracy rules. And the monarch leads. I shall be the monarch who will govern the lands that have the people with the freedom to their rights. We are also working on unlocking all the levels."

Trinity's eyes shined with pride for her mother.

Dariana spoke. "Let us summon the assembly, before you depart on your journey."

Trinity nodded. Looking at Salvos she felt herself say the words she never thought she would, "Bye, Father. See you soon."

***

Eddie yawned and sat up on his couch. He noticed that Adrian was sitting on the armchair where Trinity had been sitting before, when he was sleeping. Taking the goblet of water that sat on the pod next to the couch, he looked at Adrian with one eyebrow raised. "What? Were you staring at me when I was sleeping?"

Adrian made a face. "I'd rather watch the drainage flowing out to the lake."

Eddie snorted. "So why are you here?"

"I am a free man. I can be anywhere I want."

"And you chose to come here and stare at me."

Kryptal entered. "Dariana summoned an assembly. Trinity,

Brahanne and Sahara are leaving soon."

Adrian shifted in his seat. Kryptal came and sat next to him. Adrian said, "We will be right there. But there is something I need to talk about."

Eddie stretched his legs. "I knew it. I am not really that beautiful anyway."

Adrian ignored him and continued, "I am going on an expedition."

Kryptal spoke, "And?"

"And I need your help."

Eddie retorted, "You are known for breaking the trust of those you ask for help."

"Yes, but now you know the reason. Anyway, I do not work for the bridge any more."

Kryptal put on a deep-thinking face for a while, "Listen, I can come with you. Because I do not really have a home I can go back to and I am still not comfortable living with the other keepers, but where do you want to go?"

Adrian replied, "I want to go looking for my friend Samaar. He might not have been a highlight of our war, but he still was a helpful friend. I know he also won't be expecting anyone to come looking for him, but I want still want to do this."

Eddie said, "I mean if it involves helping someone, I am ready to come. Look at Trinity, she is risking everything to find her best friend. I will come with you, Adrian. But none of your silly tricks. Deal?"

Adrian smiled. "Deal. And that is not the only reason. I was discussing with Breeman earlier that Salvos and Reh captured so many innocent people, I hope we find them and rescue them. They are all in Village according to the information provided by Breeman."

Kryptal said standing up, "Okay, now let us not keep Dariana waiting."

Eddie and Adrian got up as well. "We can prepare to leave after Trinity and her friends leave."

They agreed to that suggestion. Eddie said while reaching the door, "So do not you think Reh and the rest like Zen and Zella will not practice dark magic in the prison? Because I am quite sure Reh appeared well aware about the dark energies back at the void."

Adrian answered, "That is the reason they have been put in a drug induced coma. And they are not going to wake up for a long time."

He noticed relieved expressions on the faces of Kryptal and Eddie as they walked downstairs for the assembly.

19.

The hall was decorated elegantly, and the essence of royalty bloomed in the air. Trinity stood there in the centre wearing leather pants with ankle high boots, a knife safely tucked in its hilt on her belt. Her green velvet shirt complimented her black leather vest on top of it. A green cape covered her shoulders. She looked ready. Sahara and Brahanne stood next to her smiling brightly dressed similar to hers. She noticed Eddie, Adrian and Kryptal enter the hall. Angelica hopped up to them with a brand-new sword in her hands. Everyone engaged in happy chatter until Dariana arrived and stood in front of the crowd. All of them faced her, now silent.

Addressing everyone present in the hall, Dariana said, "I Dariana Halo-slate, your leader, hereby declare Sandsmid as a free land. Send this in writing to all the levels." Everyone cheered, clapping loudly.

She raised her hand. Everyone became silent. Then looking at Trinity she continued, "And as for my daughter, our saviour, Bluebee, who now goes by Trinity, I declare her the knight of the armies of Lighthouse. She will be on a sabbatical for some time but shall resume her duties after she is back."

There were cries from the crowd. "Long live our saviour!"

Dariana smiled as she walked towards Trinity. The crowd dispersed into small groups scattered around the hall. "Shall we proceed to the labyrinth then?"

Trinity asked her embarrassed, "I do not know a thing or

two about battles. What were you thinking?"

"Not exactly. I remembered I trained you well for a combat," Adrian said coming up to them.

Eddie joined.

"I know, but that is different. This is an entire army," Trinity said nervously.

Eddie laughed, "You will learn everything slowly. I am sorry I called you weak when I met you. You are the only person I met with the strongest heart." Trinity hugged him. "It's okay, Eddie. Make it up to me when I come back."

"I will," he said and smiled. "Good luck on your search. I, Kryptal and Adrian are going to look for Samaar in the Village."

Trinity said, worried, "I hope he is okay. I think about him. Even though our meeting was brief, he had been extremely helpful. Good luck on your journey as well guys," she said shaking hands with both. "And thank you for being there for me in Toronto for all these years." Adrian smiled. "What are friends for?"

"For keeping their promises. I want that institute when I come back," said Sahara as she walked up to them.

Adrian laughed, "I promise. It's yours from this very moment."

Sahara narrowed her eyes. "You better be right about it."

Angelica joined. "So, thank you for all your help. I am leaving for Desert soon."

Trinity hugged her. "No, thank you for everything. I shall come visit you someday."

She smiled. "And I will wait for you. Since my father is going to be in the Lighthouse for most of the time, I need to handle the Desert affairs."

Trinity replied, "I understand. You are going to be great I

have no doubt about it."

She nodded happily. Kryptal came. "So are you thinking about visiting your world once you find your friend?"

Trinity thought for a while. "I mean I did have a life back there in Toronto. I kind of miss it. I will for sure go back there with Aella."

Adrian spoke up, "And what about here?"

Trinity answered, "I will be back here as well. You managed to stay back there and here quiet well. I will come back and learn that from you. Anyway I had a long break back in my college and I am known to leave my house and not come back for days because I used to stay at Aella's so no one would care if I have been gone for a while. And anyway, all those who care are over here," she finished.

Dariana and Haseena spoke together, "Trinity, we should leave." Trinity agreed with them. Before she could say goodbye to everyone present there, Haseena handed her a small leather bag. "Healing potions and many other ones with magical properties for your journey. They are all labelled so do not worry." Trinity replied gratefully taking them, "Thank you, Haseena. And thank you for healing me in the caves." Haseena hugged her tight. "Your mother has done a lot for me. That was nothing. Now let us go."

Trinity hugged everyone with a heavy heart and then parted ways with them. She, Sahara and Brahanne turned to follow Dariana and Haseena. Just as they were about to head out, the hall got flooded with pinkish lights. Everyone stopped and looked around. The rays of light entered through all the windows. Dariana along with the others ran to the window to look outside to see a bright pink sky showering a blissful dawn over the city that bathed in darkness for years. The people inside were still in the awe of this strange phenomenon.

Trinity smiled silently as she finally headed out of the hall with Dariana and her friends. She recalled watching the silhouettes of all the five wolves in the sky and then remembered their line in her dream, 'We shall be back before dawn'. She climbed down the stairs satisfied. The dawn the Lighthouse deserved was finally here. Their victory against the evil was obvious.

Dariana and Haseena stood with candles in their hands. Trinity, Sahara and Brahanne walked towards the labyrinth. Trinity hugged her mother and Haseena. Dariana held her face in her hands and said, "Trinity, always remember to trust your heart and not the scene." Trinity nodded and hugged her tight again. Dariana let go of her tearfully mouthing the words, 'Be safe.'

Trinity turned around followed by Sahara and Brahanne. She stepped inside the labyrinth and took a deep breath. "Aella, we will find you."

***

Samaar woke up with a start. It took a while for his eyes to get adjusted to extreme bright light. He tried to get up but noticed his hands and legs were strapped on a glass table. He uncomfortably shifted on the table and shouted, "Is there someone who can help me? Help please. Get me out of here."

He struggled but stopped when he noticed the grip on his hands only tightened when he moved. He stopped moving completely and tried calling out again, "Hello? Anyone?"

A small red hooded figure trotted up to him. It was covered in red robes. It shouted in a squeaky voice, "My bad, my bad.

Sorry man. Here let me help you."

Samaar watched as he grabbed a stool from nearby and climbed on it to open the straps. Soon they all came off and Samaar sat up. "Thanks. Who are you? And how did I get here?"

The little creature removed its hood to reveal a man with a small face and big blue eyes. They were as big as tennis balls. He looked at Samaar curiously before blinking and answering, "You had been in hyper sleep. I found you passed out by the rocks outside. No, I watched a few men dressed in armour dump you there. So, after they left, I dragged you here."

Samaar looked down at him. There was no way he singlehandedly put him on this high platform. He asked doubtfully, "You put me here?"

The creature shrugged, "I had help from my brothers. They look like me as well. Ha-ha, it's hard to distinguish us. They have gone out to search for food by the way," he added timidly and then looked down.

"But why did you tie me?"

"So that you do not fall off the platform."

Nothing made sense, however, Samaar asked him, "Yes, but who are you?"

The creature giggled. "I am Crawly. I am from Prima. Our ship crashed here, but we have kept it well hidden from the prying eyes of your people."

"Hidden? How?"

"Reflective shields. Makes it invisible to the viewers," Crawly replied.

"But why did you get me here?"

"Because you looked like you needed help. Anyway, you can help us prepare. You look stronger than us," Crawly squeaked.

"Help you prepare for what?"

"Help us against the threat that's brewing. The core of the Flux is unstable, it might explode, releasing the dark energies over your lands. And if that happens, Prima can get destroyed as well."

"Okay, Crawly, everything you said just bounced over my head. If I were strong enough to help you, I would go help my friends."

Crawly watched him bobbing his head to his side. "Help them with what?"

"Never mind. I do not even know what's going on outside this level. How long was I asleep for?" Samaar said scratching his head.

"For a few days. And do not worry, you are in our ship. So you do not have to face the outside dangers."

"But what if you are a threat?" Samaar asked furrowing his brow at Crawly.

Crawly crossed his arms at him. "Is there anything you can do about it if that's true?"

"No, I guess." Samaar withdrew.

"Good. Do not worry. We are the good guys. But these are the bad ones. I received this when I was leaving Prima. It was from one of the escapees of the Flux," he said, handing him an envelope.

It had a black wax seal bearing an insignia of a black star. Samaar opened it and read, *"We sense you. We are coming."*

***

Trinity and company had been walking for hours. The winding

of the ways kept on confusing them. Their journey so far had been quite uneventful and boring. Trinity halted for a breath glancing at her friends, "Should we rest for a few minutes?" The other two nodded exhausted.

They sat on the ground their backs leaning against the tall stone wall. They had been walking on these winding paths since like forever. The labyrinth had revealed an infinite maze with towering walls touching a dark and foggy sky. It had been exciting in the beginning but soon they were fed up with reaching a few dead ends. They had to retrace their steps again and again to walk around the boring unending maze.

"I thought it was going to be exciting," Sahara wailed.

"So did I," Trinity said as the gloom settled in. "We need to find a way that at least leads us somewhere."

"Agreed," Brahanne said.

"Can you believe it? Today is Equinox," Trinity asked smiling.

Brahanne replied, "I know. Imagine the fear and destruction."

"But thanks to our saviour we could experience an actual dawn in Lighthouse," Sahara said raising her hands.

Trinity laughed and then looked around, "Where do you think we are? Outskirts?"

Brahanne shrugged. "I am not sure. We could be in another dimension."

"But then we could experience the electromagnetic disturbance or something unusual at least," Trinity said thoughtfully.

"True," Sahara said.

"Anyway, let us get going. There are no rights or lefts hopefully. Just straight ahead," Trinity said getting up and walking again.

They walked straight ahead, and the direction appeared to be north. The air started getting colder. Trinity wrapped her cape around her. The icy feeling creeped in as cobwebs started appearing on few of the walls. Trinity could see an opening ahead of her. It was distant but clear. She started taking fast and eager steps towards it. The other two struggled to keep up with her.

Big stone gargoyles stood on either side of the way, roughly looking like winged dogs. Trinity walked past them and entered the opening and sighed. In front of her was a huge open space leading to four narrow openings to more winding pathways. Trinity swallowed, looking at her friends, "I think we reached the centre of the maze."

"I do not think so," Brahanne said pointing at the gargoyles behind them. "I think we just reached the beginning of the maze. The real puzzle is inside all of those entrances."

"How can you be so sure?" Sahara asked.

"Because these gargoyles appear to be guarding the maze. Must be my imagination but we have to choose one entrance out of those four anyway." Brahanne shrugged.

Trinity noticed a white light escape and enter the second maze from the corner of her eye. "Let us go through the second one," she said confidently. The girls followed her wordlessly, not caring particularly over why Trinity chose the second one.

They entered the second maze and after taking a few left and rights, came across a floating ball of white light. They stopped and looked at it hypnotised. After a few seconds, the ball started bouncing up and down floating towards the right of the maze. Trinity signalled the other two to follow it. They kept on following the ball for a while and stopped when the ball disappeared into thin air. It was a good thing that it was not absolutely dark inside the maze because of occasional torches on random walls.

"Now what? I thought it was guiding us or something," Sahara said.

Trinity looked around. "I think it was. See that?" She pointed at a brick wall ahead of them with bright torches. The air started subtly getting warm. The brick wall had a door on it. Trinity pushed it open to see absolute darkness inside. Each borrowing a torch from that wall, they entered the door.

The ground was starting to get uneven, with a cave formation above their heads. The caves were getting more like tunnels now with white stonework covering the ceiling.

Sahara stopped in her tracks. Trinity looked at her concerned. "What is it?"

"Trinity, look at the ceiling. It is not stonework." She flashed her torch above her head so Trinity to study the ceiling. Trinity gasped.

"It's bones," Brahanne whispered, her voice shaking.

"Should we go back?"

Trinity observed the cave thoughtfully before replying, "I have read about such a place from back in my world. It is in Paris, a city in Europe continent. It is called the catacombs of Paris. They are made up of millions of remains of people. I think we might be close to the portal gates to my world."

Sahara looked frightened. "Are you sure this is not a threat?"

Trinity waved her torch around, "Let us walk for a bit. If we sense danger, we back off okay?"

Sahara nodded looking uncertain.

They walked for a while ahead but instead of the

catacombs like the ones Trinity had predicted, their feet felt as if they were getting sunk into dry sand. A strong hot breeze caught them off guard. There were lesser and lesser bones and the ceiling of the cave sparkled in the dim light. The reflection from their torches made the cave look bathed in mild red light. Brahanne curiously flashed her torch up and her eyes grew wide.

"Trinity! Sahara! I think we should turn back now."

Trinity and Sahara turned to look at the ceiling following Brahanne's gaze. It was covered in gemstones. Ruby, everywhere. Other gemstones like emerald and sapphire showed their faces in the minimal. Now they understood why the cave glowed red. The sand began to thicken around them and far ahead, Trinity could see a bright opening with sunlight pouring in from an opening somewhere above it.

Brahanne shivered as she spoke, "I do not think it's safe for us here any more. Let us turn back now, because if I'm not wrong, this is one of the most dangerous places in Sandsmid."

Trinity asked, "So you mean to say we are still somewhere in Sandsmid?"

"Yes. And I have read about this place back when I was still on the run. I think we are in the 'Luring Moors'."

Sahara stopped in her tracks. Trinity asked them confused, "What are those?"

Sahara replied, "The darkest region of Sandsmid. I have just heard stories about it when I was young. I never really knew they existed."

"But I am seeing bright sunlight after days," Trinity argued.

Brahanne looked around fearfully. "This place has a heart of its own. It has everything that will appear pleasing to the eyes. The mirage of the deluded reality. Slowly, it will sense your presence, showing you everything you desire trapping you here forever."

Trinity thought for a while. Before she could say anything, the place ahead of them that appeared bright turned pitch black. They could still see around because of their torches and observed that now the cave appeared to stretch ahead of them. Trinity signalled the others to turn back but there were two narrow ways stretching out instead of the one they had come from, right behind Brahanne, therefore making it confusing to find their way to return. Trinity whispered, "Now what?"

Sahara replied. "The only way to stay put is to not believe everything you see."

The bones in the beginning must be of the people who must have been trapped here before, Trinity thought. But there had to be a way out of all this. After all these days, one thing she had learned was, there was always a way out. If only one remembered to trust their heart and not the scene. She asked Brahanne, "But how do you know whatever you see is real or not?"

Brahanne thought for a while murmuring something before saying it out loud, "Spare the greed, touched to please, turned to sand. Yes! So this is how this place works. The mirage always makes you think there is water ahead. The same way, this place will present to you something that your heart desires, be it food or money. But the moment you take it in your hand, it will turn into sand. But the duration of any object turning into sand increases the further you go into this place, making it impossible for you to predict what is not real, which at one point drives you insane."

Trinity called out, "Guys, stay tight behind me." They both nodded.

Trinity walked a few steps ahead but stopped when she stepped over something. Nervously she lowered her torch. It was almost dark as their torches had nearly died. Her heart skipped a beat when she realised it was not something that she had stepped over. It was someone.

"Guys!" Trinity cried in panic as her friends rushed to her. The body was facedown but Trinity recognised it immediately. Dark red hair and a tiny little body. With shaking hands, she felt her vein. Brahanne looked at her expectantly. Trinity nodded. "Still breathing."

Glad that it didn't turn immediately into sand, they carried the body to the side and Trinity watched relieved as she appeared to be in deep sleep. With her heart pounding in her chest, Trinity shook her best friend. "Aella, wake up."

Aella mumbled, still not opening her eyes.

Sahara spoke, concerned, "We need to get her out of here as well, but I do not see how."

Aella mumbled again, as if trapped in slumber, "I know a way."